Best Friend's Brother

Loving You Again

Sofia Finn

© Copyright 2021 - All rights reserved.

The content contained within this book may not be reproduced, duplicated or transmitted without direct written permission from the author or the publisher.

Under no circumstances will any blame or legal responsibility be held against the publisher, or author, for any damages, reparation, or monetary loss due to the information contained within this book, either directly or indirectly.

Legal Notice:

This book is copyright protected. It is only for personal use. You cannot amend, distribute, sell, use, quote or paraphrase any part, or the content within this book, without the consent of the author or publisher.

Disclaimer Notice:

Please note the information contained within this document is for educational and entertainment purposes only. All effort has been executed to present accurate, up to date, reliable, complete information. No warranties of any kind are declared or implied. Readers acknowledge that the author is not engaged in the rendering of legal, financial, medical or professional advice. The content within this book has been derived from various sources. Please consult a licensed professional before attempting any techniques outlined in this book.

By reading this document, the reader agrees that under no circumstances is the author responsible for any losses, direct or indirect, that are incurred as a result of the use of the information contained within this document, including, but not limited to, errors, omissions, or inaccuracies.

Table of Contents

CHAPTER 1: NATE 1

CHAPTER 2: SADIE 11

CHAPTER 3: NATE 21

CHAPTER 4: SADIE 33

CHAPTER 5: SADIE 41

CHAPTER 6: NATE 51

CHAPTER 7: SADIE 61

CHAPTER 8: NATE 69

CHAPTER 9: SADIE 79

CHAPTER 10: NATE 87

CHAPTER 11: SADIE 97

CHAPTER 12: NATE 107

CHAPTER 13: SADIE 117

CHAPTER 14: NATE 127

CHAPTER 15: NATE 137

CHAPTER 16: SADIE 147

CHAPTER 17: NATE	155
CHAPTER 18: SADIE	163
CHAPTER 19: NATE	173
CHAPTER 20: SADIE	181
CHAPTER 21: NATE	189

Chapter 1:

Nate

"Hey handsome, want to dance?"

My friend Brad nudged my shoulder and the tequila in my glass spilled over the rim, threatening to stain the sequined dress of the woman who was speaking to me. A hand flew her to mouth as she gasped, appalled that I nearly ruined her outfit.

"Sorry, what?" I asked, blinking out of my daze.

Since I returned home from my deployment, I had a bad habit of slipping back into my thoughts. I couldn't help it, not even if a ditzy blonde woman was begging me to escort her on the dance floor.

"I asked if you want to dance," she purred.

Twirling her hair in between her fingers, she batted her eyelashes, and a grin tugged at the corners of my lips. I leaned back onto the wall, relishing the attention. It had been a long time since I had kissed a girl, but I'd seen her jumping from guy to guy earlier, and I had standards to uphold.

"No thanks," I said.

Crossing her arms over her chest, she pushed up her breasts and even went as far as to give them a little shake. A tease—a temptation—one I was strong enough to withstand. Sighing, I shook my empty glass in Brad's face. "I need a new drink."

I walked around a cluster of girls in short dresses and headed for the bar, but nearly plowed over a short brunette who hovered next to the speaker. Sweat trickled down my spine, the thud, thud, thud, from the speakers reminding me too much of the sounds I heard overseas.

"I'm sorry," I muttered, grabbing the woman's elbow before she landed flat on her face.

"Oh, it's alright," she said, brushing her hair out of her face. Our eyes locked and my heart fluttered in my chest. For a second, I thought I knew her from somewhere, but her twisted expression made me think otherwise.

"Do I know you?"

"No."

The bartender whistled to get her attention. "Hey miss, your drink is ready," he said.

Blushing, she grabbed the martini glass and waved her card over the terminal. "Well, have a nice night," she said, and just like that, disappeared into the crowd.

I searched for her, but it was pointless; the club was too dark to make out any faces from a distance.

"Sir? You need a drink?"

Swallowing the lump in my throat, I nodded, holding up two fingers. "Tequila. Make it a double."

He poured my drink quickly and I downed it all in one go. It burned my throat, but I refrained from making a face. Turning the glass upside down, I placed it back on the bar and slipped into the crowd. To my luck, Brad and his friends were still talking to the blonde and her entourage.

"Hey, you!" I grabbed her by the waist and twirled her around. "What's your name?"

She giggled and placed her open hand on my chest. I hoped she couldn't feel my racing heart.

"Maia," she teased.

"Maia," I repeated, letting my hand slip down her shoulder blade until it rested on the lower back. "I'm Nate, it's a pleasure to meet you. How about that dance?"

She did not give me a chance to change my mind. Raising our linked hands above her head, she dragged me out to the center of the floor for the whole club to see.

Maia was a great dancer, swaying her hips to the rhythm of the music. She pressed her back against me and leaned in close, tilting her head up until our lips met. She tasted like strawberry lip gloss and vodka. Her hands explored my body, and even though we were in a room full of people, I did not really care.

Turning her to face me, I gripped Maia's face with both hands and sucked on her bottom lip. "Want to get out of here?" I asked.

She nodded, her eyes gleaming with lust. But before I had the chance to escort her out of the club, a tall man dressed all in black stepped in front of me.

"Excuse you," I hissed, trying to shove past him, but he stepped in my path once more.

"Dude, what the hell's your problem?" I growled.

"Are you Mr. Nathaniel Turner?" the man asked.

For the second time tonight, my heart felt like it dropped into the pit of my stomach.

The only person who used my full name was my grandfather. I took a good look at the man standing in front of me who, unlike all the other men in the club who wore t-shirts and jeans, was dressed in a black three-piece suit. His shoes looked expensive, as did the rest of him, and on his wrist was a shiny watch.

"Who wants to know?" I asked.

"Jack Turner," he replied, confirming my suspicions.

What that man wanted with me I couldn't say, but since I had only been home for a few days and his men were already hunting me down, I figured it wasn't good.

"What for?"

"He'd like to discuss some business with you, so if you'll please follow me, your presence has been requested."

I know what that word meant. *Request* was just the polite word for demand in Jack's eyes. Releasing Maia's hand, I gave her a quick kiss on the cheek. "Sorry sweetheart, duty calls I'm afraid."

She frowned, and a part of me suspected she was hoping for a wild night, but with a quick glance at the man standing in front of me, she conceded. "Another time," she said, blowing me a kiss before walking off. I hoped she wasn't about to find a new man to share her bed with tonight.

"The truck's parked out front and ready whenever you are, sir," the man said, motioning toward the exit. "Did you bring a vehicle with you? An associate can drive it back for you."

"No, I took an Uber with my friends," I said. I thought about telling Brad and the others that I was leaving, but I did not want them to see my grandfather's bodyguard hovering behind me like a shadow.

"So, what happened to Tom?" I asked.

For the first time, the man smiled. "Retired. I'm Wyatt, his replacement."

***

The drive to the mansion was uneventful. I rode in the backseat of Wyatt's SUV, the window rolled down, hoping the breeze would sober me up a bit. My head was fuzzy and my mouth was dry, and I smelled of sweat and tequila. I could already imagine the look of disappointment on my grandfather's face as I stumbled through the doors.

"We're almost there," Wyatt said as he pulled up to the gate. He punched in a code at the padlock and it slowly rolled open.

Driving up the hill toward the mansion, my knees bobbed up and down, anxious to get out of the car to get this over with. The house was the same as I remembered, perhaps smaller, since the last time I was here when I was a child. Inspired by Victorian-style architecture, delicate stonework covered the awning over the massive double doors. It was big enough to park underneath, which is where Wyatt stopped the vehicle. The siding was painted a deep blue, and there were enough windows that I surely wouldn't be able to count them all.

The car door opened and I nearly fell out of the truck. I steadied myself, and the man dressed in a peculiar uniform gawked at me, but regained his composure. "Welcome home, Mr. Turner."

"Nate," I corrected him.

I loathed formalities. I always thought it was a way for rich people to make themselves feel even more superior. In my eyes, it just made them look pretentious. I wanted to tell him that this wasn't my home either, but I held my tongue.

Walking up the short steps, Wyatt slipped me a breath mint and I silently thanked him. Another man opened the door for us, and I was greeted by the household staff, who all had fake smiles on their faces. It was late, and I'm certain they had far better things to do than stand around like a bunch of fools, but I acknowledged their effort, giving them each a handshake and a nod.

The foyer had two staircases that lead to the east and west wings of the house. With both his children and grandchildren all grown up, I had no idea why Jack still even lived in the mansion. I could only imagine how eerie it was to sleep in such an empty house.

"Nathaniel."

I looked up at the balcony between the two staircases to find Jack Turner himself standing there in all his glory. Despite his age, he looked good, his hair was gray but styled, and he wore a maroon-colored suit with brown shoes. He rested a hand on the iron railing before descending the left staircase.

"Grandfather, it's been a long time," I grinned.

There was no bad blood between me and my grandfather. It was my half-siblings that drove me away from our broken family. I would never admit it to them, but they were the reason I decided to join the army in the first place.

"Too long. The last time I saw you, you were just a boy. Now a man stands in front of me."

With a big smile on his face, he pulled me into a hug. I wrapped my arms around him in return, allowing myself a few moments of tenderness before I built my walls back up.

"Wyatt told me you had some business to discuss with me."

My grandfather looked over his shoulder at the line of household staff standing silent and attentive. "Julia, please make sure my grandson's room is ready, and the rest of you are dismissed for the night," he said.

"Jack," I urged, and my grandfather visibly winced as if I hurt him. I guess he wasn't used to being addressed so casually, but I did not have the patience to adhere to the household standards.

He turned to face me and I felt a bead of sweat trickle down the side of my face. I raised my chin higher, showing I could not be intimidated. Not any more.

"I've allowed you to travel the world with your troops long enough. It's time for you to take your place in this family, alongside your brothers. I'm getting old, and soon, I'll require a successor to take over the business, and I will not allow an outsider to steal everything I've built. This is not an option, Nathaniel. You will live in this house until I say otherwise."

Maybe it was the alcohol and lack of food in my stomach, but I felt queasy all of a sudden. The last thing

I wanted was to settle down and wear a suit for the rest of my life.

"Hello, brother."

My head snapped to the left and down the hallway, as the bane of my existence smirked as he approached our grandfather. Alexander Turner. I never liked my half-brother, nor did he have any affection toward me. I was fine with that. As long as we were civil, no one would say a thing about our indifference.

"Alex," I greeted, squeezing his hand as hard as I could.

He clenched his jaw and tried to do the same, but his strength was no match to mine. I'd been in the army for a decade while he probably sat around on his ass ordering people around.

"Benjamin's here too, and your assistant will be arriving tomorrow as well."

"Assistant?" I asked. What on earth do I need an assistant for?"

"Yes. Her name is Sadie and you'll treat her with respect."

Alexander opened his mouth to say something, but our grandfather glared at him, and he snapped his jaw shut. After a few seconds, my brother backed down, retreating up the stairs, stomping like a child.

I did not even realize that I was left there alone, as I was too busy trying to remember where I'd heard the name Sadie before.

Chapter 2:

Sadie

"Here's your coffee, ma'am. Have a great day."

The woman muttered something impolite under her breath, but I gave her my best customer service smile anyway. As much as it pained me to work not only one low-paying job but two, I did not have much of a choice. I had to pay for law school somehow.

My phone vibrated in my back pocket.

"I'm going on my break now. I'll be back in fifteen minutes," I told my boss, and quickly ran to the breakroom before the person on the other line could hang up.

"Hello?"

"Is this Sadie Thatcher?" a man asked.

"It is. How may I help you?"

"My name is Jack Turner. I believe you know my grandson, Alexander."

Know him? Alexander was my best friend! He had been ever since we were in high school. My stomach twisted into knots, fearing something might have happened to him. I stumbled to the plastic chair in the breakroom, biting the skin around my nails.

"Yes, I do. Is he alright?"

"Oh, yes, he's fine. Sorry, I didn't mean to make you worry. I'm calling because I'd like to offer you a job in our household as my grandson's assistant."

"Work for Alexander?" I blinked. I did not know if I felt comfortable following him around all day taking coffee orders or whatever it is that family did. Alexander did not like to talk about work much.

"No, my other grandson. I have three."

"Oh. Well, that's very kind of you to think of me sir, but I already work two jobs as it is, and I could never balance three while also taking care of things at home."

"You definitely wouldn't need those other jobs while employed by us. I assure you, Miss Thatcher, you'd be properly compensated."

My knee bopped up and down as I thought about never having to deal with another rude customer over a cup of coffee again.

"Can you give me some time to think about this, Mr. Turner?" I asked.

"Absolutely. But don't take too long, darling. Opportunities like this don't stick around forever."

"Yes, of course. I'll call you by tomorrow. Thanks so much."

The caller hung up and I placed my phone on the table next to me and rubbed vigorously at my temples. I had been dreaming about a big break like this for years now. I would not have to barely scrape by every month when it came to paying the bills. I could take care of Nana and the girls, and maybe even put aside a little extra for school, too.

There was no way I was going to make this decision alone though. I picked up my phone again and quickly dialed my best friend's number from memory.

"Hey Sade," Alexander chimed. I must have caught him at a good time—he was never chipper this early. "To what do I owe the pleasure of a mid-morning call from my bestie?"

"You'll never guess who just called me," I replied.

"Gerard Butler?"

We laughed in unison. "I wish. No, your grandfather! He offered me a job to be one of your brother's assistants."

There was a long pause on the other line. "Who?"

"He didn't say," I answered, leaning as far back as the plastic chair would allow and kicked up my feet on the table. "Do you think I should take it? You know how hard it's been for us these past few months. To not have to work two jobs would be amazing."

Another long pause. "I don't know, Sade. Working for my family? It might be weird. Plus, my brothers aren't like me. They'd treat you like dirt, trust me. It might be best if you just hold out a little longer where you are than to get mixed up in our drama."

Tilting my head back, I let out a deep sigh. I knew he was right. Still, I wanted nothing more than to leave this place and never look back.

"I guess so," I murmured.

"Hey, if you ever need any cash, you know you—"

"No. Remember our rule?" I warned.

"Right. No handouts. I thought I'd try. But hey, I have to run, so I'll talk with you later. Say hello to the girls for me. Love you."

"Love you too, Alex."

* * *

I stared at the ceiling in the early hours of the morning, waiting anxiously for my alarm to go off so I could start my day.

For some reason, I couldn't stop thinking about Jack's offer. I would be a fool to not accept, even if it would be awkward for the first little while to be working alongside Alex. I had to think of my family's future—my future—everything I had been working toward. This would put me one step closer to achieving my dreams.

My alarm buzzed beside me and I rolled over to turn it off. After a quick shower and putting on my dirty uniform from yesterday, I tiptoed into the kitchen only to find the light on.

I turned the corner to find Nana sitting at the kitchen table, her reading glasses on, and a piece of orange paper in her hand.

"Nana?" I whispered, not wanting to wake the twins. "What are you doing up so early?"

She looked up at me with tears in her eyes. "You're not going to be happy about this, love."

Swallowing the lump in my throat, my heart sank at the two words in huge block letters.

Eviction Notice.

This wasn't possible. We weren't behind on our rent and I always made sure to pay it on time. Even if I had to go without other things, making sure we had a roof over our heads was my number one priority.

I scanned the paper, and it said that the building had been sold and everyone was being forced to move out. I instantly started to sweat. Where would we live? There was no way I could afford a new place, not with the money I made now.

Slamming the notice down on the kitchen table, I rifled through my purse for my phone. "I have to make a call. Don't let the twins see this. Everything's going to be fine."

Nana nodded and I left the apartment and dialed Jack's number in the elevator.

"Turner Real Estate, how may I direct your call?" A woman answered.

"I'd like to speak with Jack, please."

"May I know who's calling?"

"Sadie Thatcher. He called yesterday offering me a position in his company," I replied.

"Just one moment."

I was put on hold for a whole of three seconds before the line was answered. "Miss Thatcher, thank you so much for calling back. How may I help you?"

"I'd like to take you up on your offer," I blurted. The elevator door opened, and I stepped out, heading for the parking garage. "But I have some conditions."

"I'm listening," Jack remarked.

"I require an apartment in the city."

"There's no need for that, you'll be living in the mansion like the rest of the assistants."

"Not for me, for my family. We just received an eviction notice, and they have no other place to go."

"I can agree to that. Anything else?"

"Yeah. When do I start?"

"Immediately. There's no need to go to work today. Pack your bags and I'll have a car sent over to your place this evening."

* * *

The drive over to the mansion had been fantastic.

A man named Wyatt came to the apartment to retrieve me and my belongings, along with a massive moving van and a crew of five or six men to help Nana and the girls move.

We had sat in silence the entire way through the city, and I was perfectly fine with that. I had been too wrapped up in my thoughts to carry on a conversation.

After brief introductions to some of the household staff, Wyatt escorted me to Jack's private office in the mansion.

"Sir, Miss Thatcher," Wyatt declared, waving me through the door and shutting it promptly.

Jack was handsome for an old man. His hair was silver, but styled to make him look younger. He had few wrinkles on his face and wore a black suit. I'd never met him before, and Alexander only spoke about him when he was complaining about work. Apparently, Jack was a bit hard on the boys when it came to the business.

"Come in, come in. Have a seat." He waved to the leather chair opposite his desk, and I shuffled across the room and sat down. "I take it everything is in order for your family?"

"Yes, the movers had just arrived when Wyatt came to pick me up," I said.

Jack nodded and filtered through some loose papers on his desk until he found the ones he wanted. He placed them in front of me, along with a pen.

"This is your employment contract. It has all the basics, how much you'll be compensated, the agreement of the apartment, your duties and responsibilities, insurance, the usual." He smiled and pointed his finger to the last paragraph. "And of course, the no-fraternization policy. This is a place of business, not a frat house. We do not allow any relationships to happen under this roof. Understood?"

"Yes, absolutely."

I couldn't imagine I would want to date anyone of Alexander's brothers after what he had told me about them. I signed and Jack collected the papers and left them in a tray on his desk. I assumed that it would be his assistant's job to take care of them from there.

"You may retire for the night, and I'll introduce you to my grandson in the morning. You're welcome to any room in the west wing. They all have their own private bathrooms as well."

"Thank you so much."

Gathering my things, I followed Jack's instructions and headed for the west wing. I wondered if Alex's bedroom was down this hall. Any room with the door left open was available to take. Most were closed, so I made my way down to the end of the hallway and chose the one on the left.

While the mansion had its Victorian architecture on the outside, the inside was rather modern. A king-size bed sat beneath a massive painting, and the walls were painted a crisp white. I put my purse and travel bag on the bed and took a quick look around the room before retreating to the bathroom. I'd never had a bathroom all to myself before. There was a claw foot tub in the far corner and a walk-in shower with glass walls on the other side.

Stripping naked, I stepped into the shower and turned on the water as hot as I could bear it. I lathered myself up in the body wash that was in there, letting the bubbles wash off my skin. The air smelled of peaches and vanilla, and I closed my eyes, relishing in the moment.

Reaching up, I grabbed the detachable showerhead and strategically placed it between my legs, the pressure making me moan just a little.

My entire body tingled with a wondrous sensation, and just as I was about to reach my peak, a man's voice made me freeze.

"Sadie?"

A man I thought I would never see again stood on the other side of the glass, his grin mocking me in my vulnerable moment.

I screamed so loud I thought for sure one of the household staff members was going to barge in to investigate.

"Nate?" I tried to cover my naked body with my hands, but there was only so much I could hide. "What the hell are you doing here?"

He leaned against the wall, crossing his arms over his chest, a delightful smile splashed across his face.

"I could ask you the same question. You're in my room. But please, don't let me stop your little pleasure fest. I can join you if you want."

"Get out!" I shrieked, pointing a sudsy hand to the door.

He raised his arms in surrender, but he chuckled to himself, slowly retreating out the door, not taking his eyes off me until the very last second.

Chapter 3:

Nate

I tossed and turned half of the night, struggling to fall asleep.

It was rather unusual, considering all the uncomfortable places I had been forced to sleep while serving overseas. You would think I would be fine with a rock for a pillow. It wasn't the soft mattress that was causing me such distress. It was the fact that only hours prior, the one and only Sadie Thatcher was naked in my shower.

Giving herself a little treat at that.

I smirked a little, thinking about her body dripping wet. But those thoughts quickly vanished when I remembered how I left things off with her.

We had been high school lovers and were practically inseparable. I remembered spending all my time with Sadie. Not here at the mansion, but my mother's house, before she died. It was at the funeral that I had been introduced to the legendary Jack Turner and told of our family business, and the power my grandfather wielded in one of the most popular cities on earth. But it extended far beyond our country. He owned foreign property everywhere and had built his corporation from the ground up.

I wanted nothing to do with the business, and after the heartbreak of losing my mother, I dropped out of high school and joined the army. I did not even have the courage to say goodbye to Sadie.

I had been in class one day and vanished the next.

Now she had found her way back into my life, and I had no clue how to make sense of it all. Did she tell my grandfather about us? Is that why she was here? I'd have to gauge the situation before making any rash decisions.

There was a knock at my bedroom door, and I did not move from my bed, but only threw the sheets over my lower half.

"Come in," I instructed.

Edith strolled in with a stack of fresh towels neatly folded in her hands.

"Good morning, Mr. Turner," she chimed, slipping into the bathroom first to begin her chores. "Your grandfather has requested to see you and your brothers in the dining room for breakfast."

There was that word again—request. I was beginning to hate it.

"When?"

"Now, sir."

"You'll have to excuse me, Edith, I'm slightly indecent."

She stepped out of the bathroom and I pointed to the sheet covering my body. Her facial expression did not change. She simply grabbed the dirty clothes I had draped over the chair and tossed them into the basket she brought with her.

"I'll be back in a few minutes once you're dressed. Now hurry up. You know how he hates to be kept waiting."

Groaning, I strolled across my bedroom and into the bathroom, where I splashed some cold water on my face to wake myself up. Someone had removed all the clothes I had sent over and all my shirts and pants were hanging neatly in the walk-in closet.

How had Sadie not seen all these things and realized this room was occupied?

Selecting something business casual, I dressed and made my way down to the dining room where everyone was waiting.

Immediately, my gaze fell to Sadie, who sat on the left side of my grandfather. Her black hair fell just above her shoulders, and she wore a charcoal grey dress with a high neckline; perfectly suitable for her first day. Around her neck was a delicate gold chain. I wondered where she'd gotten it from. It looked expensive.

"Nathaniel, come sit."

My grandfather pointed to the chair across from Sadie. I clenched my jaw tight and tried to act as nonchalant as possible, but knew I looked foolish.

"This is Sadie Thatcher, and she'll be your assistant for the duration of your stay. Sadie, this is my grandson, Nathaniel. He's just returned home from a deployment overseas."

Sadie extended a delicate hand over the table and opened her eyes wide. I knew that look. She wanted me to play along. So, she hadn't told anyone we knew each other.

"It's a pleasure to meet you," I purred, smirking ever so slightly at my choice of wording.

"There she is!" A familiar voice made me roll my eyes.

Alexander made a beeline across the dining room straight for Sadie. She practically sprang out of her seat and wrapped her arms around his neck, hugging him tightly. I did not know whether to laugh or punch something. I glanced at my grandfather, hoping he had put a stop to their display of affection, but he was too preoccupied with his eggs and toast to care.

Sadie let go and Alexander brushed a kiss on both of her cheeks, taking a seat next to her at the table.

"I've missed you," she said, returning to her meal as if she did not just embrace my enemy.

"Nana sends all her love, and the twins too."

I cleared my throat, and both looked up from their plates. Sadie's eyebrows pinched together in confusion, but my brother looked smugger than I had ever seen before.

"I'm sorry, do you two know each other?" I questioned, gripping my fork so tight my knuckles turned white.

"Sadie's my best friend; has been for nearly ten years now," Alexander explained. "That's how she got the job in the first place."

He casually leaned back in his chair, laying his arm across the top of hers, and she did not so much as flinch. She nibbled on a piece of toast, and the two of them returned to their whispered conversation.

Benjamin, my other brother, walked in, alleviating some of the tension in the room. "Splendid, you're all here. Now we can get down to business. Benjamin, this is Sadie, Nathaniel's new assistant. Sadie, this is my third grandson."

"Nice to meet you," Sadie smiled as my brother sat down beside me.

"You're just as beautiful as Alex described" Benjamin winked.

"Aw, that's very kind of you to say," Sadie said, before elbowing Alexander in the side and the two of them giggled like school children.

"I'm hosting a formal dinner here tonight with some potential clients, and I want the three of you to do some major mingling. I want the word to spread that my three grandsons mean business."

My grandfather closed his newspaper and stood up abruptly, readjusting his tie. "And I expect you to all be on your best behavior."

My eyes flickered to Alexander, who shockingly was already staring. I did not say a word, unsure if I would be able to keep my promise if I made it.

* * *

The afternoon consisted of awkward tension and insufferable small talk with Sadie as we got set up in Jack's office.

He had cleared an entire section on his floor for Benjamin, Alexander, and myself, as well as our assistants. Naturally, Sadie's office was much smaller than mine, but it sufficed to get the job done. A technician was called in to hook up our computers and work phones, and then it was just the two of us. For the entire day.

Luckily, it went by in a flash. We had retired from work early since my grandfather was so adamant about this work dinner he was having back at the mansion.

"Meet me in the foyer at 9 o'clock," I instructed as we returned home. "I'd like to greet everyone together if you don't mind."

"Fine," Sadie snapped, quickly retreating up the steps. I followed close behind, admiring her figure before she glared at me over her shoulder.

I gave her a playful wink, but was met with a door slammed in my face. Chuckling to myself, I went to my room across the hall and found a blue suit laid out on the bed. Rolling my eyes, I read the scribbled note. "To make a good impression, Jack."

Getting dressed took no time at all. In fact, it was too early to go downstairs. I did not want to come across as eager, and I certainly did not want to do any mingling without my grandfather around to witness. I was happy to find the house staff had heeded my request of setting up a bar cart in my room and had my pick of the lot. I settled for my usual—tequila—and poured a double before swallowing it in one go. Liquid courage. That's what Lieutenant General Mateo always said before we deployed.

I lounged in my chair as not to ruin the freshly pressed suit when there was an aggressive knock at the door.

"Who is it?" I chirped.

"Who do you think?" a female voice hollered back. "You're late. I've been waiting downstairs for you!"

Crap. I looked at the time on my phone and it said 9:31 p.m.

Scrambling to my feet, I rushed to the door and swung it open to find Sadie in a striking cocktail dress. It was maroon, complementing the navy blue of my suit. Her hair was half wavy, making it a little shorter, and she had done a smokey eye makeup look. She looked absolutely beautiful.

"Wow, that dress—"

"Yeah, save it, can we just go? I don't want Jack to think I'm ill-equipped for taming you. We have an important first impression to make."

I gawked at her, not accustomed to the backtalk. She always did have a strong opinion, even in high school. "I'm the boss, not you. We'll leave when I say so."

Her left eyebrow rose, and I thought it was better to save the bickering for my brothers. Closing the door behind me, I held out my arm and she groaned, but took it regardless.

Everyone was present by the time we entered the dining hall.

It was elegantly decorated, string lights hanging from the ceiling, and a long table taking up the center of the room. Some were already in their assigned seats, while others mingled in corners, drinks in hand. Staff members walked around with silver trays, offering hors d'oeuvres before the main course was plated.

"Sade, you look amazing," Alexander whistled, approaching us from behind.

Sadie released her grip on my arm and hugged my brother, who kissed her on both cheeks. What was with these people? They saw each other this morning; it wasn't like it had been years.

"Oh, stop it, you know I'd much rather be in sweats and curled up watching Netflix than all dolled up," she joked.

Alexander smirked as if he were pleased to be part of some inside joke. We locked eyes and his face fell flat. "Nathaniel. Nice of you to show up. Jack was looking for you, I told him to expect you'd be fashionably late."

"It's my fault," Sadie pipped in. "I didn't want to come downstairs alone, so I had Nate wait for me."

She glanced up at me, her delicate hand resting on my bicep, giving it a firm squeeze. It was her way of saying play along.

"There you are."

Benjamin strolled over with a drink in hand. He waved to the table where Jack was seated. *When did he arrive?*

My grandfather clinked the side of his glass with a fork, silencing the room. "If you would all take your places, we'll be serving the first course momentarily."

Sadie and I found our seats near Jack, and she was conveniently placed between me and Alexander.

"I take it everything went well at the office, Miss Thatcher?" my grandfather asked, taking a spoonful of soup and sipping it.

"Yes, the technician came by and set up our computers. He even gave me a work cellphone, so I wouldn't have to put any clients into my personal phone."

"Excellent. Nate, I'd like to introduce you to an old friend of mine, Ronald. He's just moved back to the city and is looking for a condo to buy. Perhaps you and Sadie can see what we have that's available."

I nodded frantically, trying to ignore my brother's childish grin. I was good at a lot of things, but business deals? I hadn't perfected that.

"Absolutely, and if we don't have anything to your taste, we'll be sure to find something and crack a deal somewhere," I replied.

"My brother knows all about making deals," Alexander murmured. "I'm sure you made lots overseas, Private."

"It's Captain to you," I hissed.

"We don't have titles here," Alexander snipped.

"Enough," Sadie warned, pinching both of us underneath the table. "Ronald, I do apologize."

Ronald nodded, and he and Jack went on to have their private conversation. I sighed with relief, but knew I would get a lecture about my behavior tomorrow when no one was around.

"I couldn't imagine coming home after serving for so long and settling back into normal society," Alexander continued, directing his conversation to Sadie. I knew he wanted me to hear it. "I'd be ashamed of what my brothers and sisters thought of me tucked away in a mansion while they were off risking their lives."

I slammed my hand so hard on the table, some of the women gasped. Drink glasses clinked against each other, and Jack glared at me, a disapproving look flashing in his eyes.

"You have no idea what you're talking about," I sneered.

With that, I tossed my crisp white napkin in my untouched soup and stormed out, the click of Sadie's heels following me out of the room.

Chapter 4:

Sadie

Jack warned me that his grandson was going to be somewhat insufferable at times, but I wasn't prepared for full-blown temper tantrums.

The worst part of it all was the fact that I knew this person—or at least, some version of him—a long time ago. It feels like a lifetime has passed since we have last seen each other and now, he has seen a little too much of me.

"I'll handle this," I whispered to Jack and he gave me a quick nod before smoothing over the rest of the room.

Alex grabbed my hand, with a pleading look in his eyes, but I did not have a choice. I was here to do a job and, as Jack informed me when I first arrived, he wanted me to reign in Nate.

"I'll be fine. I promise," I said, before chasing after Mr. Drama Pants.

When I fled the dining hall, Nate was already halfway up the stairs, bumping shoulders with some of the cleaners who were tidying up the house.

"Get out of my way!" he shouted, and the cleaner tried his best to become one with the wall. It was either that or go tumbling over the railing. What a lawsuit that would be!

"Nate!" I called out and he stopped abruptly, turning to look at me over his shoulder. "Please stop. Let's talk about this."

His bottom lip curled back into what I could only describe as a snarl. Alexander pushed his buttons—that much was obvious—but the Nate I knew wouldn't allow such a thing to happen. Whatever things he had faced in the last decade had changed him.

"Leave me alone, Sadie. Go back to the party with your best friend."

He turned on his heels and took the stairs two at a time, leaving me to clumsily chase after him in my heels. I cursed under my breath every step of the way, only stopping to apologize to the cleaner who fumbled to pick up all the linens. I wanted to offer my help, but Nate needed me more than the cleaner did.

This wing of the mansion was eerily silent. Most of the rooms were vacant besides the boys and the assistants, and since everyone was downstairs, it was just the two of us. When I reached Nate's bedroom, which was located conveniently across from mine, his door was open just a crack.

I couldn't help but wonder if it was intentional, or if in his blind rage he simply did not think to close it all the way. Weighing my options, I hoped it was a subtle invitation that he did want to talk, just not with other eyes and ears around.

Giving the door a quick knock, I opened it part of the way to find him standing at the bar cart, an empty glass in his hand.

"That was quite a first impression you made down there," I said, half-lingering in the hall. "I'll do my best to smooth things over with Ronald. You don't want to mess things up with your first client."

"I don't care," Nate spat, discarding the glass and plopping down in a chair by the window. It had started to rain, and little drops of water hit the glass. It was rather relaxing, and for a moment, I wanted nothing more than to go back to my room and have a hot bath.

Sucking in a deep breath, I walked in and closed the door behind me. "Your behavior downstairs was extremely unprofessional. You're an adult, Nate, not a child, you can't just stomp your feet—"

"I don't understand why I need to keep reminding you that you work for me, Sadie, not the other way around. You're my assistant; you take my calls, book my appointments, fill out my paperwork, and fetch my coffee if that's what I want. Do I make myself clear?"

"No," I said, crossing my arms over my chest. "I'm here to make sure you don't make a fool of yourself. Your grandfather really wants you to succeed in this business, but you're not going to do it by raging out whenever someone upsets you. Get it together."

Nate stood up and crossed the room so that we were standing only a foot apart. His breath smelled of liquor, but it wasn't strong, as if he had had a drink only moments ago. I stared at his chest, unable to meet his intense gaze.

"What makes you think I want anything to do with the family business?" he asked in a low tone.

His intensity sent a shiver down my spine. The last time I stood this close to Nate Turner, my entire life changed. Not that he knew anything about that.

"Why wouldn't you? You'd have your whole life set; you could have whatever you wanted."

"Not everything."

This time I looked up, allowing myself to get lost in his piercing green eyes. Heat burned in my stomach, traveling further down south. His chest rose and fell in rhythm with mine. We were in sync. My eyes fluttered shut momentarily, and I desperately wished we were sixteen again when nothing else had mattered in the world but each other.

"Why did you come back? Alexander said something about your deployment being over, but you could've gone anywhere—"

"My mother," he interjected.

I opened my eyes to see that his back was turned to me, as if he were uncomfortable talking about this. I did not know much about his mother, as she died before we were together in high school. What I did know was that she had passed away in a terrible accident. That's all he ever said.

"I don't understand. You came to visit her grave?"

Strolling across the room, he pointed his chin to the second chair by the window and I joined him, crossing my ankles and folding my hands in my lap. He remained silent for a few minutes, his hand resting on his face as he watched the rain fall. For a second, I wondered if he was going to speak at all.

"My mother's death was declared an accident. I was just a kid at the time, I didn't know any better, and I didn't question it. My father, our father—" He waved his hand in the air as if to motion toward Alexander and Benjamin, who were somewhere in the mansion "Wasn't around. It was Jack who raised us. Well, Jack and the nannies. When I joined the army, I was assigned to Lieutenant General Mateo's platoon. He was tough as nails, but he and Jack went way back. They were long-time friends. I'd even go as far as to say he was sort of like an uncle to me. Anyway, I always kept a picture of my mom on me while overseas. Right here." He patted his chest pocket, and I wondered if her picture was on him now. "Mateo saw the picture one day and there was something in his eyes that I'll never forget. Pain, heartache, I dare say even guilt. That's when I started to wonder if it really was an accident, or if it was something else."

I sat there for a second to digest everything he had said. "So, because of his reaction, you feel as if she was what, murdered?" It felt wrong saying it out loud. The thought alone made my skin crawl.

"I don't know," he sighed, throwing his hands up until they flopped down beside him. "But I'm hell-bent on finding out. I need to know, Sadie. That's why I'm here—to find out the truth. Even if it was all an accident, at least I'll be able to sleep at night knowing there was some dark secret waiting to be uncovered."

"I'll help you," I blurted, some piece of me instantly regretting it. This was a man I was supposed to hate for picking up everything and leaving me behind. Besides, the only reason I was here was to do a job, get paid, and get one step closer to law school. I wasn't some Sherlock Holmes detective—not yet anyway.

"Really?" He sat up taller and I did the same. "How?"

"Well, if you must know, I'm in the process of applying to law school, and I might have some connections. I've interned at a few places to boost my chances of getting accepted, so I have a few private investigators who I've worked on a few cases with. I could give them a call and see what they can do."

"Are you sure? I wouldn't want to put your career in jeopardy for my sake."

I waved my hand as if it were no big deal, even though it definitely was. "It's totally fine. Besides, it'll make me look good, dedicated. They'll see it as a bonus, not a fault."

"Alright. Well, thank you. It means a lot."

There was that look again. The fire in the pit of my stomach returned, and I was tempted to drop everything and act on it. But I couldn't—Nate was my boss, and I had willingly signed a contract forbidding it. Somehow, that made it all the more tempting.

My phone buzzed in my clutch and it was like we both snapped out of a daze. I scrambled to answer it, hoping Nate did not catch a glimpse of the caller ID.

"Hey, what's up?" I asked, my failed attempt at sounding casual.

"How's my loving brother?" Alex snickered on the other line. I had never seen him so petty before. Apparently, estranged siblings brought out the worst in each other. I wouldn't know anything about that, being an only child.

"Everything's good. I was just about to run myself a bath to unwind. Chat tomorrow?"

"Alright, don't let him drag you down, Sade. You've worked so hard; I'd hate to see it all go to waste over some guy."

If only Alexander knew Nate wasn't just some guy. She knew his concern was coming from a place of love—she trusted her best friend more than anyone in the whole world. Well, except perhaps Nana.

"I know. Let's do lunch tomorrow," I offered.

"Sounds great. My treat. Enjoy your bath. Love you."

"Love you too!"

I hung up, and my cheeks flushed as Nate glared at me from the other seat. It was obvious he did not approve of my friendship with his half-brother, but he had no say in the matter.

"If that's all, I'll see you bright and early in the morning." I gathered my things and walked to his door, and to my surprise, he followed me out.

Leaning down, his lips brushed against my ear. "Enjoy your bath. Try not to think of me while you're in there."

Chapter 5:

Sadie

There was something about working with your ex-boyfriend that made the day feel even longer than usual.

Tossing my phone, bag, and folder of paperwork onto my bed, I flopped down next to everything, rubbing my temples. It had only been a few days, but it was exhausting with all the awkward small talk, forced smiles, and tension. If I had known from the beginning it was Nate Thatcher who I would have to work in the next room with, sit beside while drivers took us to wherever we needed to go, and lived with, I don't know if I'd have agreed. Sure, the money was good, and the fact that Jack was gracious enough to give my family an apartment in the city because of my stupid landlord was a godsend, but was it really worth all this?

Despite what Nate had said about not wanting to be a part of the family business, he sure was determined to win against his brothers. We spent every waking moment making phone calls to potential clients, looking at businesses that were in danger of foreclosure, and at land that could be converted into condominiums.

What I needed was a chance to escape it all. Sadly, the friends I had from my other jobs were really only my friends because we worked together. None had reached out since I quit on the spot, nor had they answered my texts of apology, saying that I had an opportunity come up that I couldn't pass on.

I convinced myself I did not need them—but it would be nice to confide in someone who wasn't related to my boss and ex-boyfriend.

There was a quick knock at my door and Alexander entered with his hands over his eyes.

"You decent?" he asked.

"Yes," I giggled. "Come in."

He dropped his hands and had a grin from ear to ear. He quickly shut the door and belly-flopped onto my bed, sprawling out as much as humanly possible. Even though he was tall like his brother, the king-size bed was no match for even him.

"To what do I owe this honor, Mr. Alexander Turner?" I snickered, laying on my stomach next to him.

He looked as drained as I did. We barely had a chance to spend any time together, as Nate had me running errand after errand. I had a sneaking suspicion it was his attempt to keep us apart. But it was Friday night, and I was off the hook until Monday—I had a contract that said as much.

"Don't take this the wrong way, Sade, but you look awful."

I gasped and smacked him in the face with one of my many pillows. "You never tell a lady that!"

"You're no lady," he laughed, and proceeded to engage in a tickle takedown. That's what he always called it since I never had a chance. He pinned me underneath him and tickled me so much I feared I was going to pee myself.

"Alright, alright, I give!" I shrieked, and he finally stopped. He rolled off next to me and we lay there for a few minutes on our backs, our laughter never fully dying out. It was exactly what I needed.

"We should go out tonight," he suggested, turning his head to face me. "Go to a club, get drunk, and just forget about work for a night. What do you say?"

I did not even give him a chance to back out. "Abso-fricken-lutely! Where do you want to go? The Vault? Azure? We haven't been to Club Rogue in a while. That might be fun."

"Actually, I was thinking of someplace new. It just opened up and people have been raving about it for months."

"What's it called?" I asked.

"Uh, I don't remember the name off the top of my head, but I know how to get there. So, get up, hop in the shower, throw on some makeup and pick out the sexiest dress you brought. It's about to get wild."

* * *

I did exactly as Alex instructed. I washed my body from head to toe, shaved my legs and lady bits, brushed on some eyeshadow and eyeliner, and put on my shortest dress.

We weren't as young as we used to be, but I wasn't afraid to admit I still looked hot. The black dress made me look more tanned, and I paired it with some sparkly pumps. An hour and a half later, Alex and I were in the back seat of his car, singing at the top of our lungs, most likely annoying his driver.

I did not care though. I couldn't even feel the cold wind as I propped myself out the window to belt out the chorus to *Single Ladies*. Pedestrians pointed and waved, and I hollered back. Fun Sadie was back—and I hadn't even had a drink yet.

We drove through all of downtown, but we did not stop. I shifted in my seat to look in the rear window, my eyebrows furrowing. "Where is this club?"

"Just around the corner."

Alex pointed right when his driver made a left turn. We drove down a dark street with barely any lights, and the driver pulled into the packed parking lot of a giant warehouse. I tried to spot a sign that said what the club's name was, but it just looked like an empty building to me.

"This is super sketchy," I said. "Are you sure this is the right place?"

"Just trust me," he grinned, grabbing my hand and practically dragging me out of the passenger side door.

Bass thumped and I felt the vibrations in my chest. We walked hand in hand toward the building where a man dressed in black stood by a door. I would have missed him, had it not been for the flashlight he beamed in our faces.

"Names?" he asked before flashing the light at Alex. "Oh, sorry sir. Come on in." With a wave of a badge, the door unlocked, and he let us through.

I thought it was a bit odd that the bouncer knew Alex's face, and even more so that he treated him as if he owned the place. I shook my head hoping the worries and all the stress from work would go away with them.

Pushing through some velvet curtains, we walked down a flight of stairs and entered a giant room with a massive DJ stage, lights bouncing off the walls, and the dance floor packed with very attractive people. I spotted a bar at the far side of the room, and a group of girls walked by covered in neon paint.

"Hey Alex!" One of them waved. "Who's the girl?"

"This is my best friend Sadie." He introduced me, placing a hand on the small of my back. "It's her first time."

"How exciting!" she squealed, and disappeared into the crowd.

We made our way to the bar, sticking close to the outside wall so we wouldn't get sucked onto the dancefloor. As usual, we knocked back a couple of our favorite martinis and I could feel confidence rushing through my body.

It was time to dance.

"Shall we?" I offered a hand and he grinned.

"You go on ahead. I'll watch from here for a while. Just don't go far."

I gave him a little shove, but skipped into the group of sweaty bodies and a tall blonde gravitated toward me.

"You're new," he said loudly over the pounding music.

"How could you tell?" I replied.

"I would never forget a face like yours."

Heat rushed to my cheeks and we danced, our bodies becoming one. I tilted my head back and lifted my hands in the air, losing myself in the music. He ran his hands over my body, and my eyes gravitated to Alex, who was leaning with his elbow on the bar, watching intensely. My heart fluttered for a second, but I ignored it, not wanting to lose the high.

"What's your name?" he asked, nibbling at my ear. It tickled and I squirmed, but he held a firm grip on my body so I couldn't go anywhere.

"Sadie," I said. "And you?"

"Callum."

Cupping my face, he planted his lips on mine. At first, it was soft and sweet, but then something changed, and he kissed me harder, deeper, as if his life depended upon it. I hugged him closer, so there wasn't a fraction of space between us. He moaned in my mouth, and I sucked on his bottom lip before he pulled back, his lips exploring every inch of my neck.

Everything was going so well until, out of nowhere, he was violently ripped from my arms. "What the hell?" I growled, meeting the eyes of the one and only Nate Turner.

He dragged the two of us by the arms until we were out of the crowd and standing beside the bar. His face was flushed, his nostrils flared, and he looked like he was on the verge of beating Callum to a pulp.

"Who's this?" Callum snarled, pushing Nate's chest, but he did not even so much as budge.

Nate stepped closer, their noses practically touching, and it was as if the whole room was filled with testosterone. If this were a test to see who was Alpha, I knew who would win.

"He's my—"

"Boss," Nate growled, poking the man in the collarbone. "Now I suggest you go find yourself some other girl to—" He looked at me with bloodshot eyes. "Kiss, before I make you regret ever walking into this godforsaken place."

Callum retreated like a puppy with its tail between its legs. I'd never seen a man concede so quickly. To be fair, the Turner brothers had a way of commanding a room.

"Brother!" Alex popped out of nowhere, a beer in hand. "How lovely of you to join us. Wait a second, how did you find us?"

"Yeah, I didn't even know where this place was." I recalled, crossing my arms over my chest. "Are you stalking me or something?"

He motioned to the clutch tucked underneath my arm. "You brought your work phone with you, genius. It has a tracking device in case it ever gets lost. When I looked at it, it was in the middle of nowhere and I was worried something might've happened to you. Never did I expect to stumble upon this."

Nate turned to Alex, his face anything less than pleased. When they stood in front of each other, it was clear who the brawn of the family was—perhaps it was all those years in the army. Nate's shoulders were much broader, his biceps bulging. He was even a few inches taller. "The bouncer said you own this place. Does Jack know about this little underground club you're running?"

"I don't have to explain anything to you," Alex slurred. Nate shook his head before taking my hand and walking away. "Where are you going? That's my best friend you're manhandling!"

"I'm taking Sadie home before she gets mixed up in your shady business," Nate spat.

I remained silent, not wanting to get in the middle of things. I did not even yank my hand out of his grasp as we walked out of the unnamed club and into the black SUV parked out front.

He opened the passenger door for me and quickly walked around to the driver's side and sped off, creating a dust cloud in his wake.

"I'm sorry you had to see that," I said. He was the last person in the world who I wanted to catch me in such a compromising position.

We stopped at a red light and I could feel him staring at me. When I turned to face him, he reached around my neck and kissed me hard—even harder than Callum kissed me. His tongue slipped into my mouth and it was like an explosion in my body. I had wanted this for so long, I did not think of anything for those ten seconds.

My phone dinged and he pulled away right when the light turned green. I looked down to see a text message from Alex.

> (12:49 a.m.) Alex: Sorry he ruined our fun. Next time, leave the phone at home. Love you.

I sighed and turned the screen off.

"I don't want you kissing other boys," Nate said in a low tone.

I nodded, biting my lower lip slightly, the taste of him still lingering in my mouth. There was no one else I wanted to kiss.

Chapter 6:

Nate

I did not know what I had been thinking when I kissed Sadie.

It was like I had been possessed. Some greater force compelled me to do it, and there was no stopping it. The moment our lips touched, I realized she was the only woman in the world I wanted to be with. The only problem was our complicated past. I did not know if she would ever be interested in starting things up again, and I'd never put myself out there unless I was certain.

Besides, could she ever want the man who packed up and left her behind after promising we would spend our lives together? I know we were just young teenagers, but that could not have been easy to get over.

Pulling up to the mansion, I tossed my keys to Wyatt, who just happened to be standing on the front porch having a cigarette.

"Park the car please. I'm taking Sadie up to her room."

Wyatt's eyes flickered to Sadie, taking a long look at her club outfit and giving a single nod. I was prepared to knock some sense into him if he so much as made a sly comment, but he knew better. Jack would have never hired someone incompetent.

"Right away, sir," he said.

Luckily, the house was quiet at this time of night. The staff would have retired to their rooms for the night, and anyone else awake would pay them no mind. I was grateful that I had arrived there when I did—Sadie did not seem too drunk. In fact, she did not even stumble in her high heels. She walked with poise and grace, although her cheeks were a bit flushed. Besides her appearance, you wouldn't know that she had just come from an illegal club.

We remained silent until we stopped at the end of the hall, standing in front of our rooms.

"Thank you for the ride," Sadie murmured. She tucked some of her hair behind her ear and forced herself to look at me, and if I did not know any better, I would think that she was about to cry.

I took a generous step forward and brushed my thumb against her cheek as a tear began to fall.

"Sadie darling," I whispered. It was what I used to call her in high school. I pressed my forehead against hers and closed my eyes for a moment, losing myself in our wonderful memories. "Please don't cry."

"Everything's just so messed up." She sniffled. "I'm just here to do a job, so I can take care of my family and go to school."

"You're doing your job just fine," I said, cupping both of her cheeks so I could look her in the eye. "Forget about tonight, and don't worry about Alex. I'll take care of everything. Take the weekend and just do nothing and we'll start fresh on Monday. Sound good?"

She nodded, and I brushed my lips against her forehead before turning on my heels and vanishing into my bedroom. It took all my willpower to not glance over my shoulder and see if she was staring.

* * *

Sadie took my advice and stayed in her room all weekend long.

I had seen a few of the staff members coming and going from her room with trays of food, but that was it. Sitting at her desk just outside my office, she looked refreshed and ready for the week ahead.

"Good morning, Miss Thatcher." I smiled, placing a cup of coffee in front of her. "I hope you had a pleasant weekend."

"I binge-watched three seasons of my favorite show and ate a ton of food. I'd call that an excellent weekend." She smirked.

"Can you do me a favor? Call Alexander and ask him if he could speak with me in my office. I'd like to have a word about a business deal."

Sadie fiddled with her necklace and pursed her lips, but nodded, nonetheless. "Right away, Mr. Turner."

She picked up the phone and started to call his number as I headed for my office. I was thankful Jack had the good sense to separate us enough that we weren't all hovering over top of each other. Sure, we were on the same floor in the building, but Alexander and Benjamin were on opposite sides, while my and Sadie's office were in the middle, right in front of the elevator.

I had just settled into my desk when Alexander burst in without so much as a knock at the door. My lip curled in a grin, knowing his move was intentional. He was trying to establish dominance—that he did not need to ask my permission to enter my office. He could do whatever he wanted. Or so he thought.

"Sadie said you wanted to see me," he began. "What's up?"

I stood up and walked over to the other side of the room so that we weren't on opposite sides. Rolling up the sleeves of my shirt, I leaned on the edge of my desk and crossed my arms over my chest.

"You're welcome to get mixed up in whatever shady business you have going on at that underground club, but you will not drag Miss Thatcher down with you. Do I make myself clear?"

Alexander had the audacity to laugh in my face. He placed his hands on his sides and started to pace back and forth, shaking his head and mumbling under his breath. "You think you can boss me around, because you're what, a few months older? You have no say in what I do, Nate. You barely have a say in Jack's company. I've been working here for years; you've been here less than a few weeks."

I sidestepped into his path and he crashed into me. He stumbled backward, almost falling straight on his ass, but composed himself. Well, not entirely, as his nostrils flared and his cheeks turned beet red.

"Why do you care so much about what your assistant does after work?" he questioned.

"We were high school sweethearts," I admitted. It brought me great joy to watch the wheels turn in his head as he pieced it all together. That his best friend was once my lover.

"No." He chuckled, rubbing at his temples. "That's not possible. You dropped out your senior year."

"Yeah, and we were together before I joined the army. I reckon your little friendship started sometime after I left. How does it feel, baby brother? To be her rebound?"

"I'm not a rebound. We're friends, and that's all," he hissed.

My desk phone rang, and I walked backward, not taking my eyes off Alexander. I pressed the speakerphone button so he'd be able to hear everything. "Yes, Miss Thatcher?"

"Jack would like to see you and Alex in his office. He said it's urgent."

"We'll be right there," I replied, and the line clicked off.

"After you." I waved, daring him to challenge me in my own office. As expected, he conceded, storming off like a child, leaving me to follow behind with my head held high.

* * *

"Mr. Richards, these are two of my grandsons, Nathaniel and Alexander. My third is out on a business appointment at the moment."

Mr. Richards was a young man with tanned skin and stylish hair. He had a few chunky rings on his fingers, and his suit was clearly tailored to fit his body. It looked like a second skin.

"So, you must be the fresh blood. How are you liking working for your grandfather?" he asked.

Alex cut in before I had the chance. "Well, I've been here for a few years now, and my brother just returned from his deployment overseas. We're showing him the ropes."

"You served in the army?"

"Yes, sir. For almost ten years."

"Well, thank you for your service. What brought you home?"

"Just thought it was time to settle down," I lied through my teeth. "Jack was gracious enough to offer me a chance in the family business and I knew I couldn't pass it up."

"You'd be a lucky man to run all of this," Mr. Richards acknowledged. "So, shall we get down to business? Let's work some magic, Mr. Turner."

It was rather exhilarating to watch my grandfather negotiate and cut deals. They did not call him the king of property investment for nothing. He had been in the business for nearly forty years now, and I had no clue why he wanted to retire—not when it was so obvious that he enjoyed the thrill of it. His assistant came in and out of the room at the push of a button, drafting up contracts and blueprints of buildings that Mr. Richards had for sale, and lastly, Jack's checkbook.

In the blink of an eye, the company owned five new high-rise buildings in the south end of the city. I'd done as much research as I could last week and learned that real estate was at an all-time high in that district. If Jack intended to flip it, he would just have to hold out a few months and he had be able to double his money.

"It's been a pleasure as always, Jack." Mr. Richards stood up and shook my grandfather's hand, and we followed suit. "Boys, good luck. You both have a knack for the business."

Jack escorted him out, leaving Alex and I to sit in the chairs by ourselves. We remained silent for a few seconds until we knew that our grandfather was well out of earshot.

"You did well. I'm surprised," Alex said, unbuttoning his suit jacket. "You even had me fooled that you cared about our little enterprise."

"I do care," I scoffed.

He rolled his eyes and paced around the room for a minute. It was a bad habit; one I wondered if he knew he even did. Such an obvious sign that I made him uncomfortable. After peeking out into the hallway, he slipped behind Jack's desk and took a seat in his massive leather chair. He then proceeded to open drawer after drawer, his eyes wide with excitement.

"What are you doing?" I asked, eyeing the door.

"This is going to be my office soon, so I'm just getting used to the seat," he remarked.

If he thought he actually had what it took to beat me at something, he had another thing coming.

"Well, well, well, what do we have here?" He flicked through a few files in the bottom drawer and pulled out a plain-looking one. I spotted the name at the top— Nathaniel Turner.

"Don't you dare!" I jumped up, but Alex twisted in the chair, just out of reach. "If he catches you snooping through personal files—"

"He won't." He slammed the folder shut, and if I did not know any better, I would have thought that he looked paler than he did just seconds ago. He quickly put it back in the same place he had found it, before slamming it shut and joining me on the other side of the desk where he belonged.

I stared at him closely, watching as he breathed in and out methodically as if trying to calm his heart rate. What was in my file that had him so freaked out?

"You two made me so proud today," Jack said, startling us both. We readjusted in our seats so we were sitting tall, not hunched over like two teenagers who were called down to the principal's office.

"It was nice to see you in action," I remarked, earning a rare smile from my grandfather.

"I want you two to each close a deal by the end of this week. At least half a million dollars. Think you can handle that?"

Handle that? I would double it. Alex and I looked at each other, and I knew he was thinking the same thing, even if he was still a little shaken up from reading whatever was in that file. The game was on.

Chapter 7:

Sadie

After the underground club fiasco and Nate's spontaneous kiss on the ride home, everything in the mansion had been mostly quiet.

The brothers were working like a well-oiled machine, closing deals and making their grandfather proud. I had even had a few lunch dates with Chloe, Alexander's assistant. She was nice enough, or at least she faked it quite well. She was a few years younger than Alex and I, fresh out of college. She had only been working for the family for less than a year, but she knew the ins and outs of the company like the back of her hand.

Alex had assured me that I would be smart to be her friend. I wasn't entirely sure what he meant by that, but I had taken his advice, and so far, it was working out splendidly. Plus, it was nice to have a girl to talk to. I was starting to miss Nana and the twins terribly.

The phone calls and FaceTime sessions were nothing compared to the real thing. I stared at a picture of the four of us on my laptop screen, lost in a daze.

"Your kids?" Chloe asked.

I nearly jumped out of my skin, not realizing someone else had joined me in the conference room early. Jack liked to hold midweek meetings with all of us together so he could get updates and information on whatever we had lined up that week. It was proactive and apparently served the company well.

"Oh, no," I stuttered, opening Google so the picture would disappear. "They're my younger siblings."

"They're adorable," she cooed, sitting a few seats down in her usual spot. "How old are they?"

"Ten," I said. Not wanting to answer any further questions about my mysterious family, I busied myself with some unanswered emails to pass the time.

As if to save me from an awkward conversation, Nate strolled in, two coffee cups in hand. I flashed him a polite smile and flicked my eyes to the seat between Chloe and me, hoping he would get the message.

After a brief hesitation, he pulled out the chair and took a seat, placing a cup by my laptop. "The usual. Vanilla latte, piping hot," he murmured.

I fetched it greedily, the delicious aroma instantly lifting my mood. Chloe let out a quiet snort and both of our heads snapped to attention.

"Is something funny?" Nate inquired, tilting his head, obviously not amused.

"No, Mr. Turner." Chloe's eyes widened so much I thought they might fall right out of her skull. "It's just that, Alexander usually has me fetching the morning coffee, not the other way around."

"Miss Thatcher does enough for me. It's not a requirement to fetch beverages," he seethed, turning his body away from her and focusing on my computer. "Any updates from our pending clients?"

I scrambled to pull open a few documents, slightly caught off guard by his scolding, although a piece of me did appreciate it.

"Miss Hodson has requested a private meeting with you on Friday, and Mr. Lewis emailed a contract for you to review. I've already taken the liberty of printing it and putting it on your desk."

"Wonderful," Nate beamed, leaning back in his chair and sipping his coffee.

No less than a minute later did Jack and Alexander walk in with Benjamin only a few steps behind.

"Good morning all," Jack said, taking his place at the head of the table. "First order of business. Nate and Sadie are the top sellers and buyers for this week, so congratulations to you both. Keep up the good work."

Nate smirked at Alexander from across the table, and his cheeks flushed pink. I brushed my leg against him under the table in hopes that it would comfort him. His gaze landed on me and we shared a brief moment before he nodded in gratitude.

Glancing away, I realized Nate was practically burning a hole inside the side of my skull with his stare. "What?" I whispered, not wanting to disrupt Jack's conversation with Benjamin and his assistant.

"Are you providing sympathy for the enemy?" Nate muttered back. There was a playfulness to his words, as if he and his brothers were kids and this was all some backyard competition.

"You forget he's my best friend."

"I forget nothing, Miss Sadie Thatcher, and not because you are constantly reminding me of such an arrangement."

I wished for nothing more than to be able to stick my tongue out at him, but knew it would be wildly inappropriate. I settled for pinching his bicep and he swore under his breath, causing us both to giggle.

"I have a proposition," Alexander declared. The room fell silent, all eyes on him. He waved for Chloe to pass over a folder, and she did so without a word.

"Go on," Jack encouraged.

"I think we should invest in a local business. The owner has posted several pleas on social media about a sponsorship from a major company, and I believe we would be a perfect fit. Not only would it demonstrate our loyalty to the community, but we'd also get a percentage of the profits of his corporation."

"Sounds like you've done your research," Jake said. Putting on his glasses, he motioned toward the folder and Alexander reluctantly handed it over. "So, what's the business?"

"Adam's Auto Repairs on Fifth Avenue."

Jack slammed the folder shut and I flinched at the force of his hand on the table. "Absolutely not."

Something in the room changed—the aura, the tension—it swirled around, turning everyone's moods. All except Nate's. He looked more puzzled than upset.

"Jack, he needs our help," Alexander persisted, despite the furious look on his grandfather's face.

"I will not hear another word about this! Do you understand me? I will not do business with that man. Not now, not ever."

"What's the issue?" Nate asked. "Have you had a deal fall through with him before?"

"And then some," Jack grunted.

He pushed himself out of his seat and snapped his fingers. Wyatt, who always shadowed Jack wherever he went, grabbed the folder, and tucked it underneath his arm. I stared at it, wondering what secrets it held.

"If no one else has anything to contribute, this meeting is over. Alexander, I'd like a word with you in my office. Now." Jack raised his eyebrows and Alex stood up abruptly, following him out.

Nate and I shared an awkward look before packing up our things and heading to our designated area.

"Is there anything you require of me right now?" I asked Nate, before he stepped into his office. "There are a few things I have to tick off my list this morning, but I can squeeze something in, should you need it."

Nate fiddled with his tie briefly before shaking his head. "No, you get to work. I'll read over this contract and if everything looks good, I'll sign it and you can fax it before the end of the day."

"Sounds good."

I retreated to the cubicle that had become my safe space in the office. The four walls around my open office gave me a bit of privacy, and since working at the company, I had taken the liberty to make it feel a little less drab. Besides my desktop computer. I had a few photos printed and framed; one of me and the twins, and another of Alex and me from when we were younger.

Just as I had started to make my way through a call list Jack had emailed me, Chloe popped into my little cubicle, startling me for the second time this morning.

I clutched my heart, and she pressed her lips in a thin line, guilt washing over her face. "I'm so sorry, I really should make some noise when I approach you. Has anyone ever told you that you scare easily?"

"No," I hissed. "But perhaps tying bells to your shoes wouldn't be such a bad idea."

"Can we talk?" she blurted. "Privately?"

"Right now?"

She gave a single nod and extended her hand for me to take. I hesitated, looking over my shoulder at Nate's closed door before grabbing it. Practically ripping my arm out of my socket, she dragged me to a wall of unused offices, slipping into one at random and closing the door behind us. I stepped in to turn the lights on, but she stopped me.

"What's this all about Chloe?" I questioned. Was she upset by the way Nate defended me about coffee this morning? Surely something so small wouldn't wind her up this much. Her skin was flushed, her silk blouse sticking to her skin as if she were drenched in sweat. No—this was something else.

"Adam's Auto Repair," she whispered, not taking her eyes off the door. "It's not just a local business."

That much was evident, based on Jack's outburst. But what did that have to do with me? "And?"

"Adam Turner is the owner. Turner, as in—"

"Their father," I wheezed.

Nate never talked about his dad, mostly because he had never met him. He had run out on his mother when she was pregnant. I had never asked Alexander about his father either, mostly because I was afraid that he would find out about my dalliance with Nate when we were teenagers. From what I knew, he wasn't a good guy.

"Why does Alexander want to fund his business, after everything he's done to him and his brothers?"

"I'm not supposed to say anything, but Alex mentioned that Adam had reached out recently, hoping to make amends for his past. He's in a rough place right now, and I think that he caught wind of the brothers working for their rich grandfather. He must've figured they'd have money to spend."

"That's not so terrible," I murmured. "If he wants to try and be a father now, some effort is better than none, isn't it?"

"No," Chloe hissed. "Adam is bad news, Sadie. I'm talking about being a borderline criminal." She leaned in close, her breath tickling the side of my face. "I found a police report from the day Nate's mother passed away. He was at the scene of the crime and gave a statement about the accident. Does that sound like a coincidence to you?"

I swallowed hard, my throat suddenly feeling dry. I desperately needed a drink of water—something— anything. If not for my firm grip on Chloe's arm, I was sure my knees would have given out.

"Who else knows?"

"No one. And you can't tell a soul. Not even Nate. Promise me you'll keep this between us?"

I nodded and she sighed with relief. As much as I wanted to run straight to Nate and blurt out the news, I knew if I did, it would crush his heart. No, this was something I had have to think about before I ruined his life.

Chapter 8:

Nate

I sat in the plush chair by my bedroom window, the untouched tequila swirling in my glass every time I readjusted.

Something had been off about Sadie ever since we left the office. Her skin looked paler than usual, and her eyes were clouded and glossy. I asked her if she had fallen ill and required a trip to the doctor, but she assured me that everything was fine. I knew my Sadie. She was hiding something; secrets were never her thing. Honesty was always the best policy in her eyes. I'm not sure if I completely agreed, although secrets did have the power to weigh a person down, especially one as good and kind as she.

"You look positively dreadful," Alexander snickered.

My head snapped in his direction, and he was leaning most of his weight on my doorframe, his arms crossed over his chest. He still wore the suit from earlier, although the jacket was long gone, and his crisp white shirt was now wrinkled and untucked from his pants.

I did not recall hearing a knock at my bedroom door. Perhaps I had left it open. My mind felt like a jumbled mess.

"What do you want?" I sneered.

My brother took it upon himself to come in uninvited, slumping down in the second chair by the window. I observed him carefully, noticing the dark circles under his eyes, and the fact that he hadn't shaved in a few days. I scratched at my chin subconsciously, the roughness a familiar feeling. For a second, I was transported back to my life across the sea, fighting alongside my comrades. Alexander cleared his throat, and I came back to reality.

"Did you say something?" I blinked, shaking my head hoping to rid myself of the dreadful feeling.

"I said Jack is a fool if he doesn't take the business deal that I proposed this afternoon," Alexander repeated.

"Why is that?"

"These are changing times, Nate. I know that better than anyone. I've been working for the company the longest. Trust me, I know what I'm talking about. We can't just focus on elite companies or millionaires anymore. Expanding our horizons to the middle class is the next step to global domination."

"You sound like a villain from a movie."

He made a face at me and I laughed. For a second, so did he. It almost felt like we could be brothers—not just by blood, but a true kinship.

"You know what I mean. One of us will become his successor, and we have to think about the future in a logical sense."

Was I losing my mind or was Alexander making a bit of sense? "Can we get to the part where this involves me somehow? With you, there's always a catch."

Alexander smirked and snapped his fingers before pointing at me. "Always such the blunt brother. There's no beating around the bush with you. Alright fine, I want to go down to that business right now and cut a deal."

"Behind Jack's back?"

"He'll thank us for it later. So, what do you say? Still think you're the rebel child or has the mansion changed you for good?"

Abandoning the tequila on the side table, I stood up and readjusted my tie. "Let's go."

* * *

Alexander offered to drive, and in less than half an hour, we pulled into a dirty parking lot on the other side of town.

A red sign with the words Adam's Auto Shop hung above a bay door, and just to the left, was a glass door that was caked in dust. I glared at my brother and he nodded his head, reading my mind. This was the place. Why Alexander was so keen on investing in this company was beyond me. It did not look like it had a customer in years.

"So, what's the plan?" I asked, wanting to make sure we were both on the same page.

Alexander pulled out a folder from the center console, and after a quick glance, I saw that he must have had his assistant draft some contracts and business packages. He was serious about closing this deal.

"Let me do the talking," he mumbled, getting out of the car.

I followed suit, but snatched the folder from his hands and grilled him when he tried to take them back. "I don't think so. I'm taking the lead; you can stand in the corner sucking your thumb for all I care."

I was not the submissive type.

"If you insist," Alexander smiled.

Tucking the folder under my arm, I walked into the auto shop office with purpose. A woman sat behind a desk, typing away, not even lifting her head as the bell chimed above our heads. It wasn't until I cleared my throat that she glanced up.

"Oh! Hello," she greeted, her cheeks flushing a rosy pink at our presence. "Can I help you with something?"

"I'd like to speak with the owner," I explained. "Is he in?"

"Yes, his office is just through those doors," she muttered, grabbing the landline and pressing a button before putting the phone to her ears. "There are two gentlemen who are here to see you. Can I send them in?"

After what I assumed was a *yes, go ahead*, the woman hung up. The hallway door buzzed, and she waved us through without another word.

"Are you sure you want to do this?" Alexander whispered as we approached Adam's office.

I scrunched my nose at his words, offended he thought I would ever consider backing down. "What do you take me for, a coward?"

"You're right," Alexander mused. "Sorry I asked."

I knocked on the closed door a few times with my knuckle. "Come in," said a voice.

As I stepped in, he swiveled in his chair to look at us, but his gaze immediately fell on Alexander. His shoulders dropped, his lips slightly parted, and his eyes were so wide I wondered if they might fall right out of his skull.

"Alex? What are you doing here?" Adam wheezed.

He remained glued to his seat. He did not even stand to greet us. I thought that was odd, as every other time I have made business deals, it was common courtesy to stand and shake hands.

"You know this guy?" I questioned.

"I'm his father," Adam said slowly. He raised out of his seat, his face paled to a ghostly white. It took a few seconds for the words to even register in my brain. "Who are you?"

"He's Nathaniel, but he goes by Nate for short," Alexander grinned. "I don't think you've had the pleasure of meeting your eldest son." My brother turned to me, slapping an open hand on my shoulder. "Nate, this is Adam Turner, our father."

Our father.

Never in my wildest dreams had I ever imagined this day would come. The day I would come face to face with the man who abandoned my mother when she was pregnant. How did Alexander even find him? How long had he been in communication with him? By the look of disgust on Adam's face, I could only assume that they weren't on speaking terms.

"You knew," I growled. Slamming my brother against the far wall, I tucked my forearm under his throat and pressed as hard as I could. "You set this up on purpose and I want to know why."

"Get off him!" Adam screamed.

He tried to yank me by my arm, but he was no match for my strength. Turning my rage onto the person I loathed most, I released my hold on my brother and punched Adam in the face as hard as I could. He flew backward, hitting the desk hard, and crumbled to the floor. Something came over me—anger, betrayal, grief—perhaps all of the above.

I wanted nothing more than to pummel this man into the ground. For all I knew, he deserved it—he left my mother and now she was dead.

"Nate, please," Adam cried, curling up into a ball on the ground and shielding his head with his arm. "I'm your father! Don't do this!"

"You're no father." I spat in his face. "You don't deserve to be called that. All you did was get mom pregnant and then left her."

"I didn't even know she had a son," Adam lied.

"Bullshit!" I screamed.

Grabbing the front of his shirt, I lifted him half off the ground and punched him again and again. His tears blended in with the streams of blood gushing out of his nose.

"Can we get some security in here?" Alexander shouted into the hallway, but even then, I did not stop—not until a large man in a black uniform pried my hands off of my father.

Everything became a blur as the guard dragged me down the hall and through the front office, where a police car outside bathed the entrance in multicolored light. Out of nowhere, cuffs wrapped around my wrists and I was shoved into the back seat of that police car.

Glancing out the window, Alexander stood with his arms crossed over his chest, and if I did not know any better, I would think that he looked rather pleased with himself. He wanted this to happen—wanted me to make a fool of myself so he would have a better chance of becoming Jack's successor.

And I fell right into his trap.

My thoughts ran in circles as the police officer drove to the station. The men tried to talk to me, but I don't remember what they said. Before I knew it, I was patted down, cleared, and tossed into a holding cell.

Luckily, it was just me in there, with a single guard sitting at the only desk in the room. He looked young, probably fresh blood in the station. He side-eyed me a few times, and I could tell I made him nervous.

"Hey, don't I get a phone call?" I stood as close as I could, white-knuckling the cell bars.

"Yes," he stuttered, "we recommend calling a lawyer."

"That won't be necessary."

The officer unlocked the cell, cuffed me again, and brought me to the desk. I assured him I was no threat, but he said it was protocol.

There were lots of people I could have called; Sadie was my first thought, but there was no way I wanted her to find out about this little incident. I'm sure she would find out eventually—in fact, I'm sure Alexander was already on his way back to the mansion to inform his best friend about how much of a monster I was.

Dialing the only number that I knew by heart, I put the phone to my ear and prayed he would pick up.

"Hello?"

"Ben," I sighed with relief. "I need a favor."

"What's up?"

"I need you to bail me out of jail."

There was a short pause. My heart thumped, and I prayed he wasn't corrupted by our brother, Alexander. "Well, that's certainly a first, even for you. How much is this going to cost?"

"I don't know. Grab my credit card from Sadie, but don't tell her what it's for. I don't really want her to worry about me."

"Alright, I'll be there within the hour. Do I even want to know where Alex is?"

Just hearing that traitor's name made my blood boil. "No," I hissed. "He should be eternally grateful that it was our father's face I beat in, and not his."

I heard Ben gasp. "Say no more, brother. I'll be there."

Chapter 9:

Sadie

"It just doesn't make any sense."

I sat cross-legged on my bed, trying with all my might to listen to Alex's story. When Ben had come by earlier asking for the credit card, I had just assumed something extravagant had caught Nate's eye. Never in a million years did I ever think he would attack another person.

"I told you he was bad news, Sade," Alex sighed.

I pulled the throw blanket over my shoulders, wishing it would offer me more comfort than it did. Surely this would not bode well for Nate's chance of becoming Jack's successor. But it put my employment in jeopardy as well. I was forever grateful that Alex's grandfather had been so generous as to offer me a position in his company, let alone take care of the rest of my family while I was away. What would I do without them? What if Nate went to jail?

I rubbed my temples and squeezed my eyes shut. "But why were you guys there in the first place? Didn't Jack say he wanted nothing to do with that man's business?"

I played it off as if I did not know Adam was their father. Chloe had told me that in confidence; unless Alex told me flat out that he knew what I knew, I was going to pretend otherwise. I definitely wasn't going to bring up the fact that I was having some of my former associates do some digging into Adam's relationship with Nate's mother, and if they found any connections to her death.

"Oh, that," Alex flinched. He twiddled his thumbs in his lap, and his knee bobbed up and down as he sat on the edge of my mattress. "Nate wanted to do a followup. You know him; if Jack tells him not to do something, he wants to do the complete opposite."

Sweat trickled down the sides of his face despite how cold my room was. I knew in my heart he was lying, but a part of me did not want to believe it. Why would Alex lie straight to my face? What did he have against Nate?

The door flew open, slamming against the wall, and a tiny yelp escaped my lips. Nate stood in the doorway, looking a little disheveled, his eyes bloodshot, but he wasn't looking at me. He was staring at Alex, his lip slightly curled back into a snarl. He looked positively barbaric.

"I'd like to speak to Sadie alone, if you don't mind," he said slowly, not taking his eyes off his brother.

Alex stood up, holding his arm out to shield me. I wanted to laugh. Nate would never hurt me.

"How the hell did you get out?" Alex demanded.

"It's none of your concern. Besides, I already spoke with Adam's lawyer and he's not going to press charges.

It seems your little stunt didn't work out as best as you hoped."

"I don't know what you're—"

"Sadie," Nate cut him off. "Can we speak privately? Please?"

Alex loomed over me, and for the first time in ten years, I did not recognize my best friend. It broke my heart.

"Alright," I said softly. I slipped out of the blanket and Alex caught my wrist, gripping it tightly.

"Don't do this," he pleaded. "Remember everything I've told you."

Reaching up with my other hand, I cupped his cheek and he sank into my touch. His eyes even fluttered shut for a second. "I'm a big girl, Alex, you don't need to protect me from everything."

With that, I joined Nate in the hallway, and Alex stomped after us, pushing Nate up against his bedroom door. "If you so much as lay a finger on her—"

"I would never hurt Sadie, she knows that. Now get out of my face before you force my hand."

Alex looked at me and shook his head in disappointment. He did not say another word, but simply retreated down the hall and slipped into the first door by the stairs. He slammed it for good measure, but neither one of us reacted.

"I'm sorry I didn't call you," Nate began. "Will you let me explain everything?"

I nodded, and together we walked into his bedroom, closing the door behind us. I stood in the middle of the room, watching him intensely as he paced back and forth in front of his bed, one hand on his hip. I did not pry. Instead, I waited for him to find the words.

"He ambushed me. I'm sure you figured that out already, but I don't know what lies he told you. I did not know who Adam was. I did not know he was our father. If I had, I never would've gone. Do you really think that's how I wanted to meet my dad for the first time? On a fake business deal? No wonder Jack did not want us to do the investment. He was just trying to protect me."

He furiously ran his fingers through his hair, messing it up slightly. When he turned to face me, his eyes looked red and puffy, as if on the verge of tears. In all my years of knowing him, I don't think I had ever seen Nate Turner cry. Perhaps this might be a first.

"I believe you," I blurted, and he stopped dead in his tracks.

His hands unflexed at his sides, and he released the tension in his shoulders, allowing them to drop slightly. "You do?"

"Of course I do." I advanced on him, sliding my hand into his and squeezing it tightly, hoping it would prove my words were honest and true. "You're not the monster he thinks you are."

"I was so worried that you'd hate me once you heard what I'd done."

Our fingers entwined, and he stood taller now, our toes practically touching. "I'm not sure I fully agree it was the best move to beat your father into a pulp, but I understand. Especially after you told me that you think he might've been involved in your mother's death."

I stopped myself from saying something that I couldn't take back. As much as I wanted to tell him what Chloe told me, I knew I couldn't—at least not until I did a little investigating myself. There was no point breaking his heart over a silly coincidence.

"I miss this," he admitted, catching me off guard. His face twisted, and a part of me wondered if he even meant to say it. I took a step forward, urging him to continue. I wanted to hear the words more than anything in the world. "Us. You. Do you know how hard it's been for me the past few days? Watching the love of my life strut around with my half-brother, the bane of my existence? Don't even get me started on that night at the club."

"I'm surprised you didn't knock him out," I smirked, tucking a few stray hairs behind my ears. Slowly, we gravitated closer to each other, as if the universe desperately wanted to bring us back together.

"Believe me, I wanted to."

"I regret it. Kissing him. I only did it because I needed a distraction, someone to get my frustration out with."

"Frustration?" He cocked an eyebrow, and I could have sworn he flexed his muscles a bit.

"A girl has needs," I mused, and his cheeks flushed. "Especially when they live across the hall from their ex-boyfriend, who is so gorgeous, it's annoying," I laughed. "We probably shouldn't even be talking like this. I do have a contract that prohibits me from engaging in sexual relations with you."

"I know," he said quickly. "Say the word and we'll stop."

He inhaled deeply, his chest rising and falling in rhythm with mine. Passion and heat burned between us, and I know he felt it too. I could tell by the way he looked at me, or rather, my lips. Seconds felt like minutes, and before I could convince myself it wasn't a good idea, I pounced on him.

Our lips met and he moaned in my mouth, his tongue swirling against mine. He fumbled to run his hands against every inch of my body. One hand grabbed a fistful of my hair and squeezed it, making me press harder against him. The other hoisted me up effortlessly and I wrapped my legs around his waist. Our kisses turned from those of hesitation to one of pure greed. We wanted each other—immediately.

Nate took a few short steps before throwing us onto the bed. His lips trailed down the side of my neck before he fumbled with the buttons of my blouse. I hadn't even changed out of my office clothes yet. He moved with lightning speed before ripping my shirt open, exposing my newly purchased pale pink bra.

Matching his desire to remove his clothing, I undid his buttons as quickly as I could before he removed his shirt himself, exposing his rock-hard abs. A decade serving overseas did wonders for his physique, and his lip curled into a grin as he caught me gawking.

"Like what you see?" he murmured.

"Just shut up and kiss me."

He obliged without further question. Yanking my skirt off, he tossed it across the room and went to work on undoing his pants. They were off in a flash, and we were back to kissing. Deep, intense kisses, and his hands cupping my breasts, his thumbs swirling against my nipples. I moaned, arching my back, pressing into him. He was hard and rubbed himself on me before removing my panties and discarding them with his boxers. Tugging on the straps of my bra, he exposed my breasts and ran his tongue in circles around my nipples, sucking on them gently as I ran my nails down his back.

Just as he was about to enter me, he stopped, and our eyes met.

"You're mine," he said in a low tone.

I nibbled on his bottom lip and he squeezed his eyes shut. "I'm yours."

Nothing would ever match the pure ecstasy of him sliding inside and the gentle thrusts building until he finished inside me, and I was left with my entire body trembling. He collapsed down beside me, breathing hard, covered in a thin layer of sweat. I thought I heard him say something, but I couldn't make out the words. I was too wrapped up in the pulsing between my legs, and how much I craved him. He turned his head to look at me, and after catching his breath, he climbed back on top and we began again.

After a night of built-up passion and desire, I lay there in the dark, watching him sleep. He looked so peaceful, so at ease, I couldn't help but think about the past. A few tears escaped my eyes, and I had to convince myself that one spontaneous night of sex wasn't going to make up for the fact that he left me behind.

I would not allow it.

Chapter 10:

Nate

After a night of pure bliss, I was utterly disappointed to find my bed empty in the morning.

I had rolled over hoping that a beautiful young woman would be fast asleep, and I could curl up next to her, perhaps sleep in a little while. I hadn't done that in so long. Unfortunately, Sadie Thatcher was nowhere to be seen. Her garments had been retrieved from the floor, and only the faint scent of her shampoo remained on my pillow. I hugged it close to my chest for comfort.

I don't know why I expected otherwise. I had broken her heart all those years ago. Last night was spontaneous and I wouldn't hold it against her if she had doubts. Besides, there was the matter of Jack's contract that prohibited such relations to even take place. I guess it was a good thing she slipped away in the cover of darkness. If someone were to find her naked in my bed, I know for certain she would be sent away. And that's the last thing in the world I wanted.

No, if this little arrangement were going to continue, and I prayed that it would, Sadie and I would have to be careful. From what I had learned upon her arrival to the mansion, Sadie was a strong, independent woman, but had struggled financially. She needed this job, and I wouldn't be the one to put that in jeopardy.

Luckily, it was the weekend, and that meant we had two days we could just hang out without any office talk. Crawling out of bed, I lost myself in all the ideas of what we could do to pass the time. Maybe I would take her for a walk down by the pier and we could feed the ducks. Or have a private tour of the museum downtown. She always loved art. At least she did when we were in high school. I froze for a second, realizing the Sadie I knew ten years ago might not be interested in the same things now.

I stood in front of the mirror and was appalled by my appearance. Who knew the love of your life could drive you mad?

"Sir," a female knocked on the door. "Are you decent?"

"Come in, Edith," I called, yanking a t-shirt over my head.

She strolled in with her basket in hand, right on schedule. Humming to herself, she went about gathering all my clothes from the hamper, and some that had been strewn about after late nights at the office. Or in this case, a crazy wild night with my ex-girlfriend.

"Breakfast is being served downstairs as we speak," Edith said. "Jack's been called away this weekend on business and he wanted me to tell you that you're in charge of the household in his absence."

I smirked and ran my tongue over the front of my teeth. Me? In charge of the household? That meant I had one step above my brothers. This was a good sign. Perhaps my setback with Adam and getting arrested hadn't made its way to Jack's desk yet. Or, if it did, he did not care. It was obvious he held no feelings for my father in his heart.

"Excellent," I purred, heading for the door. "I'm sure Alexander and Ben will be ecstatic when they hear about that."

"They already know, sir."

Even better. I did not even have to say the words to gloat. Just my mere presence will drive my brother to the brink of insanity.

"Edith, would you mind doing the bedding today as well?" I said, just as I opened the door. "But not the pillows."

She gave me a perplexed look, but did not say a word. I had made it three steps down the hall when Sadie's bedroom door opened, the morning sun gleaming all around her. She looked like an angel who had just stepped out of heaven. It took me a few seconds to realize I was just standing there gawking at her, looking like a complete fool. Blinking profusely, I cleared my throat and continued down the hall and she was quick to match my stride.

"Good morning, Mr. Turner." She smiled. I could have sworn she gave me a small wink. "I take it you slept well?"

"Best sleep I've had in years," I replied.

We both giggled as we made our way down the stairs, her hand brushing up against mine for a few electrifying seconds. "It's a gorgeous day outside," she continued. "Perhaps you wouldn't mind joining me to get some fresh air? Sometimes the mansion can feel a bit confining."

I nodded eagerly, surprised on the inside at how quickly she had wrapped me around her finger. Not that I minded.

Voices echoed from the dining hall, but before we could round the corner, Sadie pushed me into the little alcove, her body pressed against mine. I gasped, not just from the air escaping my lungs, but from how forward she was being. We could be caught at any moment—this was such a risk—if someone saw us in such a state, they wouldn't know what to do. I instantly swelled just thinking about it. Our eyes locked, and she slowly trailed her hand down my chest until she stopped right below my belt, her tiny hand cupping my manhood.

"I trust you're going to keep our little dalliance a secret?" she whispered.

"Yes."

"Good," she pushed off me. "If you behave, there may be plenty more to come."

With that, she tucked her hair behind her ear and turned on her heels, vanishing into the dining hall. I took a few seconds to collect myself, readjusting my pants, hoping no one would see my bulge. Once the situation was under control, I found my two brothers seated side by side and Sadie across from Alex, already digging into her plate.

Alexander's eyes flickered between the two of us, and he squinted in disapproval. "Good morning everyone," I said, sinking into the chair opposite to where Jack normally sat.

They all murmured their greetings, but returned to their breakfasts without further hope to carry the conversation. That was perfectly fine with me.

Simon, one of the chefs who worked on the weekends, entered with my breakfast in hand. He had quickly memorized my order when I first arrived at the mansion. Sausages, eggs, toast, and a small bowl of fruit on the side. The aroma made my stomach gurgle.

Gently putting the plate on the mat in front of me, he gave me a single nod before handing Sadie a tall glass of orange juice.

"You look positively radiant today, Miss Thatcher," Simon beamed. I snapped my head up, my ears turning hot.

"Oh! Why thank you." Sadie blushed. "That's very nice of you to say."

"I was wondering if you'd like to go out for dinner sometime. Or perhaps an evening stroll? I'm finished today at five o'clock."

I wanted to take my fork and stab him repeatedly with it. Sadie gave him an awkward laugh, her gaze falling to me as if begging me to do something about this.

"That'll be all, Simon," I growled. "I'm sure there are some dishes that need washing."

I did not relax until he had left the room. Feeling someone staring, I turned back to the table to find Alexander, my charming, psychotic brother, grinning from ear to ear.

* * *

After the breakfast incident, I noticed that Sadie was in low spirits, so I decided that spending the day away from the house was the best plan.

She loved the outdoors, so we spent the afternoon hiking different trails in the area and ended up down by the pier. I sat in silence watching Sadie as she stared out at the open water, her mind somewhere else. I desperately wanted to ask her what she was thinking about, to see if she was on the same page as I was. But when her hand had slipped in mine and she scooted closer, I had the answer I needed. This time, I vowed, I would not ruin anything by rushing or making rash decisions. If Sadie was indeed my one true love, there was no force in the world great enough to tear us apart.

So, for perhaps the first time in my life, I did not take charge and just simply followed her lead. There were a few stolen kisses on our way back to the mansion, and she had been smiling so much, she complained that her cheeks were sore. I took it as a good sign that maybe, if

I played my cards right, this wasn't just some fling. That I might actually have a chance.

"All that walking has sure worked up an appetite," Sadie said.

We had just pulled into the long driveway and she was already taking off her seatbelt, preparing for a mad dash to the dining hall. I parked in the garage, not bothering with the valet service.

"What are you in the mood for?" I asked as we slipped in through the side door unnoticed.

She stopped for a second and tapped her chin with her index finger. "Steak. Oh, and roast potatoes. And a nice green salad on the side." Her love of food always made me chuckle. For such a small person, Sadie could eat the same amount as I could. Perhaps even more.

"Anything else?" I grinned.

"A tall glass of red wine, please."

"I'll put the order in right away." Lightly brushing my lips against her cheek, I motioned toward the dining hall, telling her I would be back in a minute.

The chef on duty took down our requests and I made my way back to the dining hall where a series of voices floated into the hallway. There was one in particular that made the hair on the back of my neck stand. And for once, it wasn't my dear brother.

Simon sat next to Sadie, his hand lazily draped across the back of her seat, while the two of them engaged in a conversation with Alex. The three of them looked in my direction as I approached, but only Sadie seemed to be bothered by his closeness.

"The chef's preparing your steak just how you like it," I said, yanking out the chair beside Alex and staring daggers into Simon's soul.

"Thank you," she murmured.

"So, Sadie was just telling us that you guys went on a hike. How outdoorsy of you." Simon shifted in his seat, but his arm remained glued to Sadie's chair. "I must admit, I didn't take you to be a man of adventure."

I couldn't refrain from snorting in disgust. "You do realize that I spent the last ten years serving in the army? The majority of that was, get this, spent outside."

Simon's face turned beet red. "Right. How foolish of me to forget."

Sadie rifled through her purse and let out a loud sigh. "Ugh, I think I left my phone in my coat. Please excuse me, I'll be right back," she said, sliding out of her chair and retreating out the door as fast as she could.

"Yeah, and I need to take a piss. Be right back," Simon stated.

The room fell to silence, as there was nothing in the world that I felt like discussing with my brother. It wasn't until I heard loud, desperate whispers that something clicked in my brain. Scrambling out of my chair so fast it was knocked over, I sprinted down the hall to find Simon pressed up against Sadie.

"Simon, please," Sadie begged, turning her face to avoid any kisses from landing on her mouth.

Growling, I grabbed Simon by the back of the shirt and yanked him off with one swift motion. I shoved him against the adjacent wall, using my body as a barrier between him and Sadie.

"What's going on?" Alex gasped, only a few steps behind me.

I did not even look at him. My attention was focused solely on the scum that had his hands on my girl. "Take Sadie upstairs, I'll tell one of the staff she'll be eating in her room tonight."

Surprisingly, Alex obliged without question, and it broke my heart to hear the soft cries coming from Sadie.

"Please, sir. Let me explain—"

"You are dismissed from this household," I barked. He was lucky I had a lot riding on becoming Jack's successor, or otherwise, I would've pounded his face into the marble floor. "I expect you to be packed within the hour. I'll have security escort you out."

Chapter 11:

Sadie

It had been unsettling watching Simon be escorted out of the mansion that night.

I had stood by my window, hidden in the shadows of the curtains, the lights dimmed low. Alexander was kind enough to leave me be, and after hearing many things break across the hall, I had thought it was best to leave Nate alone for the night.

Simon had been a nice enough guy from what I knew about him. He had been rather quiet and reserved. I did not understand where this sudden urge to pursue me came from. I had been grateful that Nate had come to my rescue when he did. I may be fierce and independent, but sadly, my strength does not match that of a 6-foot-tall man. Who knows what would have happened?

A week had passed, and the mansion resumed its usual rhythm of things. Jack was absent most days, and I suspected he was planning something. When I tried to ask Wyatt about it one night, he gave me a solemn look, but did not answer any of my questions. Something big must be going on, but no one knows what.

Sadly, it's not my place to pry. In the office, Nate and I acted as professional as we could, although we did sneak a few kisses and touches here and there. I can't explain why, but there's something about the secrecy about it that makes it so hot. Slipping into the broom closet for a heated make-out session or pressing me up against his office door and copping a feel while dropping off some paperwork was exhilarating.

By the time the weekend rolled around, we had both reached our peak and demanded sexual release.

Rolling off of me, Nate sprawled on his back, tucking an arm underneath his head to prop himself up. I pulled the duvet over us and snuggled in close, laying my head on his chest. His heart was still racing, as was mine, and it was the only thing I could focus on.

He gently brushed the hair from my face and my eyes fluttered shut. It was still early; in fact, we hadn't even gone down for dinner yet, but I was perfectly content with falling asleep right there.

My phone rang suddenly, frightening the life out of both of us. I scrambled to grab it from the nightstand and made a face at the caller ID.

"Alex!" I answered cheerfully and Nate grumbled under his breath. "What's up?"

"You'll never guess what's in town," he replied. The wind whistled in the background and it sounded like he was driving.

"What?"

"A carnival! You remember how much we loved going to those when we were teenagers. Look, I was thinking, the girls could use some fun this weekend, and I wanted to check with you to see if I could take them. It'll be my treat as their favorite uncle."

"You're their only uncle," I snickered, sitting up in bed. "Yeah, I guess that would be fine. They absolutely adore you. Let me call Nana and let her know that you'll be stopping by."

"Fantastic. Hey, you should join us! It would be just like old times. Besides, I haven't seen you have fun in a while."

I glanced over at Nate and he cocked an eyebrow. I wondered if he had been able to hear our conversation—it wasn't like Alex was quiet. We were supposed to be going on a date tonight, and I did not know how he would feel about a sudden change of plans. Besides, a part of me was scared for him to meet the girls. I had never introduced them to any of my boyfriends before, not that they would know anything about Nate and me. But the thought of it made me queasy.

"So," Alex probed, and I realized I had been silent for over a minute. "Sure. Yeah, that sounds great. If you pick them up, I'll meet you there. Just text me the address."

"Wonderful!" Alex cheered. "I'll see you in an hour. Love you, Sade."

"Love you, too."

I hung up and pulled the sheets completely over my head, letting out a groan. "What is it?" Nate asked.

"Change of plans," I said, still hiding beneath the duvet. "We're going to a carnival instead. Alex offered to take Nora and Sarah and has invited us, well me, but it'll be us, to tag along."

I poked my head out when the bed shifted, only to find him getting dressed. He did not look even remotely mad, and I had no idea what to make of it. "You're fine with this?"

He smirked as he buttoned up his jeans. "I love kids and carnivals. Besides, I've been wanting to meet your sisters for some time now."

"Right, sisters," I murmured.

* * *

Bright lights glowed all around us.

They looked extra vibrant against the night sky. The pier was crowded with couples and families, so Nate and I had to zigzag our way through the carnival grounds to find Alex and the girls. He told me to meet him by the hot pretzel stand—our go-to food of choice when it came to fairs and festivals. I hadn't told him that Nate would be tagging along, and my shirt clung to my back, as I perspired in anticipation of an argument on the horizon.

I spotted the twins from a mile away and couldn't help myself.

Abandoning Nate, I ran as fast as I could in their direction, dropping to my knees and pulling them into a big hug. Tears pricked my eyes and I squeezed them tight. The girls' little giggles were the most pleasant sound I had heard in my entire life. I barely had the chance to see them since I moved into the mansion, so tonight felt like a gift from above.

Pulling away, I grabbed Alex's hand and he nodded, knowing I was grateful to share this moment with them.

"Nora, Sarah, there's someone I'd like you to meet."

Nate stood a few paces back, but when I waved him over, he approached us with a big smile on his face. Alex's top lip quivered slightly, but he quickly recovered, as if he did not want to make a scene in front of the girls. He dropped to a knee so that he was at their eye level and extended out his hand, which looked enormous compared to theirs.

"This is Nate Turner. He's an old friend and my boss at my new job."

"Are you Uncle Alex's brother?" Nora asked.

She was the more talkative one of the two. Sarah was shy and only opened up once she felt comfortable around someone. It would take some time for her to warm up to Nate. She reached up and grabbed Alex's hand for comfort. He had been around the girls ever since they were born. They loved him dearly.

"I am," Nate smiled. "We share the same father, but not the same mother."

"We don't know our dad," Nora blurted.

My heart skipped a beat. Nate tilted his head to the side, and I could tell he wasn't sure what to say to that. Standing back up, I clapped my hands to get the girl's attention.

"Who wants to go on some rides?"

"Me!" they said simultaneously, and we all laughed together. "Uncle Alex already bought us the carnival passes so we can go on any rides we want!"

"Well, the ones we're big enough for," Sarah explained.

"That was very nice of him, I hope you said thank you." I gave Alex a playful look and he brushed it off with a wave of his hand. He always loved to spoil them.

"They were angels about it, as usual," Alex beamed. "Come on. Who wants to go on the Ferris wheel?"

They squealed and each took one of Alex's hands as he led them toward the colorful wheel that was closest to the pier.

"They're adorable," Nate whispered as we trailed behind. My cheeks burned, and I was grateful for the cover of night, so he did not see.

"Yes," I breathed. "I raised them as if they were my children. Their father—" I choked on unexpected tears. "Walked out on them before they were even born."

Nate shook his head in furious disappointment. "I know the feeling. But they seem to be doing fine. I've never seen this side of Alex before, he's so good with them."

"He's been around them since they were little," I explained. "He's probably the closest thing to a father they've ever had."

With Alex's back turned to us, Nate snuck a quick kiss on the side of my head. "We'll see about that."

* * *

After the girls had a chance to go on every ride twice and stuff their faces full of junk food, we were nearing the end of our unexpected family outing.

"Hey! Why don't we do a couple of games before heading out?" Nate suggested.

The girls' eyes lit up with excitement, but turned to me for permission. "Can we, please?"

"Don't you think it's a little late, Sade?" Alex leaned in, hoping they wouldn't be able to overhear he was planning to end their night short. "It's past their bedtime."

"A few games won't hurt. Besides, look how much fun they're having." I batted my eyelashes at him and knew he would cave instantly. His lip curled into a grin and I clapped along with them. "Alright, but only a few, and then it's time to go. I just have to go to the kiosk and take some cash out."

"No need." Nate whipped out his wallet before either of us could. "My treat. Alex was kind enough to pay for the rides. I'd be more than happy to escort these wonderful girls around the game tent."

Nora shrieked, grabbing Nate's hand and guiding him to the entrance of the tent. Sarah also joined in and skipped along the other side of him just so he could keep up. My heart swelled at the side of the twins bonding with Nate. It was something I never expected to happen.

"You two are becoming quite cozy," Alex murmured, bumping shoulders with me. I looked sideways at him, and it was evident he was clenching his jaw to refrain from saying anything more.

"He's easy to get along with," I replied.

"I guess it helps that you two used to date." He said it so casually that, for a second, I wondered if I had imagined it. I stopped, and he did too, a look of disappointment washing over his face.

"He told you?"

"A while ago," Alex confirmed. "The question is, why didn't you tell me?"

I felt myself deflate under his heavy gaze. "I was embarrassed. How would you feel admitting that you're working for your ex-boyfriend? One who left overnight and broke your heart?"

My chin trembled and it took all my strength to keep myself together, if not for me, for the kids.

"He doesn't deserve you, Sade." Alex's hand slipped in mine, and for the first time, it felt like it might be something more than just a friendly gesture. It felt like I had stepped in concrete, unable to move—or escape. "He's a wanderer. He'll never settle down and be the man you want or need. Once this competition is all over with Jack and he's left with nothing, he'll leave. Surely you know that."

I did not, but it was what I was most afraid of; the thought that kept me up at night.

"He's different now," I said, swallowing the lump in my throat. "Besides, it doesn't matter. We're just—"

"Friends?" Alex raised an eyebrow and shook his head. "You can fool everyone else, but not me. Just promise you'll be careful."

I nodded, unable to form any words.

"Uncle Alex!" Nora barreled toward us with a giant teddy bear in her hand. Sarah was not far behind with a matching stuffed animal. "Look what Nate won us! He's beat the record at the balloon pop and the ring toss."

"Wow!" he gasped. "What a great way to end the night. I think it's time to get you ladies home to bed, don't you think?" Sarah yawned, and so did Nora. That was proof enough that it was time to call it quits. "I'll take them home. You two go on ahead. I'll text you once I've dropped them off."

"Thank you," I said, kissing Alex's cheek.

They disappeared into the crowd, and as I looked up to thank Nate for being so good with the girls, I noticed he was watching them too. If I did not know any better, I thought he looked heartbroken to see them go.

Chapter 12:

Nate

Sadie's feeble attempts to silence her moans with a pillow always drove me into a frenzy.

She did not want the house to hear her intoxicating pleasure, but I did. Flicking my tongue a few more times between her legs I slid up her body and ripped the pillow from her grasp, kissing her entire upper body.

She grabbed fistfuls of my hair and arched her back, closing the gap between us. She was so wet I could slip inside her with no issue at all, but I did not want to rush this. No, I wanted to relish every electrifying second, even if I had come close to finishing several times just from the mere sounds of her enjoyment. I was rock hard, and as her hand trailed down to grip me, a muffled moan escaped my lips as I nuzzled my face between her breasts.

"What are you waiting for?" she purred.

Positioning myself between her legs, I cupped her sweet face between my fingers, and she opened her eyes just as I thrust inside her. She tilted her head back and moaned once more, and I was in danger of coming. There was something about being the source of satisfaction for the woman I love that made my insides turn to mush. Unable to hold back a second more, I lost myself in the heat of the moment, and the rest of our lovemaking became a tantalizing blur.

* * *

Weeks had passed since the night of the carnival, and Sadie and I had settled into our routine of sneaking about.

We could barely keep our hands off each other, both alone and in the presence of everyone else. At night, we would stay up and ensure that everyone had retired to their rooms for the night—both my family and the rest of the household—before she made a mad dash to my room. For hours, we would get tangled in the sheets, exploring every inch of each other's bodies.

It was agonizing being at work. People were coming and going constantly; if not my brothers, clients coming in to make business deals, and of course, Jack checking in on progress. Sadie's cubicle sat directly in front of my office and it was such a tease, knowing I had to get through eight hours before we would be reunited again.

We would steal glances every now and again, a few seconds longer than normal, and my mind would wander to all the wonderful things I was going to do to her later. Sometimes my brothers would leave early on Fridays and Sadie would come into my office and one thing would lead to another, and I would end up having my way with her.

One time, I pressed her up against the wall so hard, the clock fell off and smashed to bits. We had laughed so much that we had to stop. Luckily, no one mentioned the missing clock.

Today was just like every other day. We returned home from the office an hour ago, and after dinner, it would just be a few short hours before Sadie would be joining me in my bed.

A knock at my door interrupted my naughty thoughts. "Who is it?"

"Wyatt, sir. May I come in?"

"Yes, of course."

My grandfather's bodyguard opened the door and only took a few steps. I closed my laptop so he could have my full attention. "What is it?" I asked.

"Jack has requested your presence in his private office downstairs," Wyatt explained. "He said it was rather urgent."

"Did he mention what it was in relation to?"

Wyatt shook his head.

"Alright then. Tell him I'll be down once I read through this contract," I said. I was about to open my laptop back up, but Wyatt cleared his throat. "Is there something else you require of me?"

"He said it was urgent, Mr. Turner. He meant now."

Swallowing the lump in my throat, I got up from my desk and followed Wyatt out, my mind reeling over all the possibilities of why my grandfather would want to see me so urgently. Was it possible that Adam had indeed charged me after all? Had Alex spread some lies about me?

I barely remembered the walk downstairs until I was let into Jack's office and found Sadie sitting in one of the two chairs opposite him. I stopped short, my heart beating wildly in my chest, and suddenly, this felt like an ambush. Before I could retreat, Wyatt closed the door behind me.

"Have a seat, Nathaniel." Jack motioned to the chair beside Sadie.

She looked absolutely terrified. I wanted to comfort her, but knew now was definitely not the place to do so.

"What's this about?" I asked, hoping to gauge the situation before I admitted to something that he did not know.

"We're going to be mature adults about this," my grandfather sighed. "I'm only going to ask this once. Are you, or are you not, in a relationship with Miss Thatcher?"

I twisted the ring on my finger, my leg bouncing involuntarily. He would never ask such a thing unless he knew it to be true. My eyes flickered to Sadie, and silent tears streamed down her face.

I laughed, hoping to come across as casual as possible. I even crossed one leg over my knee, but that was mostly to stop him from seeing how nervous I was. "Jack, what in the world would ever make you think something like that?"

We stared at each other for a few beats before he reached down and opened a drawer in his desk. Pulling out a file, he laid it out on the table, but did not open it. "Are you aware there are security cameras in your office?"

I swore if my heart beat any faster, it would come flying out of my chest. "No."

"I thought as much. Well, once a month I have them serviced to make sure they're in working order, and the data gets uploaded to our server. I have Wyatt take a once-over of the footage to make sure nothing in the office has been tampered with."

Squeezing my hands into fists, I inhaled and exhaled slowly, trying to keep my cool. I dared a look at Sadie, who was staring shamefully at her hands in her lap. Tears stained her skirt.

Jack continued. "Now, I'll save you the humiliation of showing you the footage that he found, but you know as well as I do why you've been summoned here."

"It wasn't Sadie's fault," I blurted. Jack glared at me, his nostrils flared, and I knew he would never look at me the same way. "I came onto her. Blame me. Don't punish her, please."

"Nathaniel," Jack leaned back in his chair and rubbed at his temples. "You know as well as I do that's not the case here."

"I'm so sorry," Sadie sobbed.

Jack's face changed to one of mournful understanding more than resentment. Plucking the handkerchief out of his suit jacket, he leaned forward, and she took it gratefully, wiping the makeup from underneath her eyes.

"Miss Thatcher, it pains me to say this, but I'm going to have to terminate your employment, effective immediately."

"No!" I shouted, jumping up from the chair and slamming my hands on the desk. Jack narrowed his eyes, and his mouth twisted most unusually. "Please don't do this to her. I'll do anything, just don't fire her."

"She broke the contract. My hands are tied, Nathaniel," Jack explained. "I have few rules, but this is one I cannot overlook." He turned his attention away from me and focused on Sadie, who was trying her best to stop crying. "I'll give you the rest of the night to have everything ready for the morning. Unfortunately, that also means you'll lose out on the other benefits that we arranged at the start of your employment. I'm sure you know what I'm talking about."

"No, no, no," I mumbled, watching my life slip away before my very eyes.

Sadie did not even look at me. She sniffled, placed the handkerchief on the desk, and excused herself without another word.

I stared at the door for a minute, hoping I would be able to get my feelings in check, but everything was spiraling out of control. The fury burning in the pit of my stomach had turned into a raging fire just itching to be let out.

"How could you do this to her?" I seethed, unable to look at the man who practically raised me.

"She knew the risks, as did you," Jack said.

This time, I looked at him, studying every expression on his pathetic face. He did not even look fazed. As if he did not just ruin both of our lives.

"We aren't just some dumb kids messing around, I—" my voice cracked, but I held my ground. I would not show weakness, least of all in front of him. "I love her. I'm in love with her."

"Will you please sit so we can have a level-headed conversation about this?" Jack asked. Obviously, he did not know me very well.

"No," I barked. "Now I'm asking you as your grandson to please make this right. Don't ruin her life over something as stupid as this."

"What would you have me do, Nathaniel?" His voice rose just a bit, and I could tell he was on the brink of anger. "If I had caught Alexander and Chloe in the same predicament, what would you say?"

"This is different, and you know it! Sadie and I, we have a history together, it's not just adult lust, it's love."

"Oh, I'm aware of your past," Jack muttered, tossing the file folder back in the desk drawer and slamming it shut. "It doesn't change anything."

I hesitated for a second, absorbing his words and what they meant. "What did you say?" My head tilted to the side, and suddenly, everything came together. The only way he would have known about Sadie and I was if someone had told him. It wasn't something he would find on any record.

"I said, it doesn't change anything."

"No, the part about you being aware of our past," I growled. "Who told you?"

Jack stared at me for a few beats before breaking eye contact first. "It doesn't matter. You should count your blessings that I'm not dismissing you as well."

"Oh, there's no need," I laughed, the kind of laugh that brought chills to a man's spine. "I quit. Good luck with Alex as your successor. We both know he's had it out for me ever since I arrived." I reached for the door handle, but stopped. "You want to know something? This is the exact reason I wanted nothing to do with you or the family business in the first place. All you care about is getting to the top, not the people you step on to get there. I feel sorry for you."

With that, I stormed off, nearly plowing over Wyatt in the process. I vowed in my heart I would never step foot in this wretched place again. Not after what Jack had done to my Sadie.

Chapter 13:

Sadie

There were several knocks at my bedroom door throughout the night, none of which I had the strength to answer.

I'm certain most of them were Nate—I swore I heard his voice on the other side—but I did not move from my bed. Alex called my phone multiple times and even sent a few long texts asking what was going on, but they went unanswered. I packed my closet, toiletries, and whatever little things I had lying around in my suitcase and rolled it by the door. The rest of the night I tossed and turned, crying into my pillow. My entire life was ruined. But I wasn't crying over that—it was the girls I was worried about. No doubt, Jack had meant that we would have to give up the apartment now. I was grateful he had the decency to be sly about it in front of Nate. I did not need him to worry about us anymore. I had gone ten years without his help; I'm sure I could do the rest on my own, too.

Morning finally rolled around, and this time, it was a woman who had called out to me. Edith, I assumed, for she always came in to do some tidying up just as I was leaving for work.

"Come in," I sniffled.

She frowned and came right over to me, sinking on the mattress and rubbing circles on my back. "Hush. Everything will be alright, I promise."

Edith reminded me of Nana. They had that same gentle touch that somehow made the world feel less broken and scary. I would miss her terribly.

"No, it won't." My chin trembled, but I had no tears left to cry. I had run myself dry.

"Wyatt's just outside. He's come to bring your luggage down. I'm afraid it's time to go, my dear." Edith brushed the hair out of my face and gave me a soft kiss on the forehead.

She helped me sit up and used her thumbs to wipe away the stray tears on my face. "You're a strong girl, Sadie; the strongest I've seen walk through those doors in a while. Don't let this break your spirits. The world needs people like you."

With that, I gave her one last hug and opened the door to let Wyatt in. He looked different today too, and a part of me wondered if he was sad to see me go.

"I'll bring this down and pull the car around," he muttered. "Take as long as you need."

I stepped into the hallway and stood in front of Nate's bedroom door, staring at it for what felt like hours. Finally, I found the courage to knock, but there was no sound from inside. I knew Nate was a light sleeper, so it was most unusual for him to not even stir.

"Nate?" I called out, knocking again. "Are you in there?"

With only silence on the other side, I twisted the knob and pushed the door all the way open. The room was a mess, the duvet was bunched up on the floor, chairs knocked over, and the bar cart smashed to bits. But that wasn't what shocked me. It was the fact that it was stripped of everything he owned.

Nate Turner had up and left in the middle of the night, just like he had ten years ago. I did not think it was possible for my heart to break even more, but apparently, I was wrong. Leaving the door wide open, I walked down the stairs with my chin held high, ignoring the house staff stopping to stare as I left the Turner mansion for the last time.

Wyatt stood at the bottom of the steps, the passenger door open and ready for me to climb in. I gave him a quick nod before sliding in and buckling my seat belt. He closed the door gently and walked around to the other side before putting the SUV in drive.

I watched the mansion in the rear-view mirror, and despite all efforts, tears fell from my eyes once more. Unexpectedly, Wyatt handed me a few tissues, and I tucked them into my sleeve, knowing I would need them.

"For what it's worth, I'm sorry you had to go," he mumbled.

"Me too."

"He loves you. I'm not just saying that because I heard him scream it at the top of his lungs yesterday, but I could see it in his eyes. I hope things will work out between you two."

I knew Wyatt meant well, but he did not know the whole story. He did not know that two wonderful girls were waiting for me at home and that this wasn't the first time their father had up and abandoned us.

* * *

Walking through the apartment doors was surreal.

Nora and Sarah pounced on me and I crumbled to the floor with them, cradling them in my lap. Nana watched us from the kitchen with tears in her eyes. I held them for hours, rocking them back and forth. This had been the first time that I had been apart from them, and it was all for nothing. The weeks I spent at the mansion, working for Nate and Jack, separated from my darling daughters, proved useless.

If only I had the good sense to set boundaries, perhaps none of this would have happened. But who was I kidding? I fell for Nate just as hard as I did in high school. Sadly, I feared the repercussions this time around would be much, much worse.

After putting the girls to bed, I came back to the kitchen and Nana handed me an all-too-familiar-looking note.

"I found this slipped into our mailbox when I got up this morning," she sighed. "We have to be out by the end of the week."

I covered my face with my hands, not wanting to cry for the hundredth time today. I had to be strong for Nora and Sarah. Now was not the time to break down.

"We'll get through this. We always will," I whispered. I wasn't sure if it was Nana I was trying to convince or myself. "Let me make a few calls."

"Sadie, it's okay to feel a little broken right now. Let me help. You shouldn't have to bear this all on your own."

"They're my responsibility," I hissed. "They're my children and I'm not going to let them suffer because of my foolishness."

"No, but their father might be able to help," Nana said.

I glared at her, my eyes red and puffy. She knew better than to bring up my romantic situation. "He doesn't even know about them, nor will he ever," I spat. "Excuse me."

Refraining from stomping all the way to the bedroom they had set up for me, I closed the door behind me and flopped face-down onto the bed. I cried for a little while, letting it all come out before mustering up the courage to make the phone call I had been dreading.

Dialing his number, I put the phone to my ear and waited.

"Hey, Sades," he said quietly. "I'm so sorry about what happened."

"Word travels fast around the mansion," I whined. "How much do you know?"

There was a pause on the other end. "The gist of it."

"You know I don't like charity, but I'm desperate and need your help. Jack is throwing us out of the apartment that he rented for us, and the girls need a roof over their head."

"Say no more. I have a few condos a few blocks from where you're at right now. They won't even have to change schools."

I sighed with relief. Alex was always there for me when I needed him. I wish all the Turners were like that.

"Thank you," I whimpered, hugging a pillow tight to my chest. "You have no idea how much this means to me."

"I love you, Sades. Don't worry about a thing; I'll take care of everything—the movers, the rental truck, the apartment, all of it. I'll see you at the end of the week."

"I love you too, Alex."

* * *

Alex was true to his word.

At the end of the week, he arrived at the apartment with a team of movers and assured us that we wouldn't have to lift a finger. Plus, he brought coffee, which was basically the only thing I had been surviving on the past few days.

"You're an angel sent from above." Taking the cup greedily, I took a generous sip and felt the warm liquid travel down my throat.

"I appreciate the compliment," he smiled, kissing both my cheeks before hugging the girls. "I told them to do their room first so we can make our way over to the new place and get everything set up."

"You are a smart man, Mr. Turner." I snapped my fingers and gathered the odds and ends I wanted to bring over first. "Shall we head to the car then?"

"Yes, and I promise you're going to love this place."

"Nora! Sarah! It's time to go!"

Nana had gone to her friend's house for the weekend for a much-needed vacation. I had been the one to suggest it, knowing the stress would not be good for her. Besides, she had been the primary caretaker of my kids for weeks, and I wanted her to have some time to herself.

The girls bounced out of the rooms and jumped into Alex's arms. "Hi, Uncle Alex!"

"Hello, my darlings. Are you all ready for your new apartment?"

"Yes!" they squealed.

He led the way, and just as he had mentioned, the drive over to the new place was quick. In just a few blocks, we arrived. The day was organized chaos, but with the help of six or seven men, they brought everything over in just a few truckloads. Alex and I got to work unpacking the girl's rooms and then the kitchen, and by the end of the night, we were completely wiped.

"Wine?" I offered, holding up a bottle of merlot and two glasses.

"Yes please," he grinned, his eyes lighting up at the sight of alcohol. I did not blame him; it had been a long day.

After pouring two generous-sized glasses, I plopped down next to him and rested my head on his shoulder. We stayed like that for a while, and I was just about to fall asleep when he cleared his throat.

"I'm sorry about my brother, Sade. I did try to warn you."

"I know. I should've listened. I don't know why I thought this time would be different."

My chin trembled and tears spilled onto my cheeks, but I made no effort to wipe them away.

"I'll promise I'll never leave you like he did. I swear on my life."

He kissed my forehead and I put the glass of wine down and sank back into the couch. "You're the best friend a girl could ever have."

Placing his arm over my shoulder, he hugged me close, and after everything I had been through the past week, I fell into a dreamless sleep.

Chapter 14:

Nate

Out of all the scenarios I had played out in my head, Sadie leaving the mansion, and subsequently my life for good, never made the list.

Not once had she tried to contact me since that awful afternoon in Jack's office. My mind drifted to the last words I heard her say.

I'm so sorry.

What did she have to be sorry for? Our love had been rekindled, restored, revived—there was nothing wrong with that. I should have fought harder, should have tried to cut a deal with Jack. After all, he was a man who dabbled in deals his whole life. Surely there could have been something to do besides sending her away.

The more I thought about it, the more I wanted it all to go away. I had barely remembered frantically packing up what few things I had of mine in that room. Of course, I'd tried to talk to Sadie numerous times throughout the night, her soft cries breaking my heart piece by piece. But she needed her space and I respected that. As it turned out, I needed space from the Turner family too.

Just as I had ten years ago, I grabbed as much as I could carry and slipped away in the cover of night, running away like some sort of coward. I had convinced myself that I wasn't, that I was doing this for Sadie's sake, but that wasn't the whole truth. How could I face Jack after he had ripped apart what was left of my life? How could I stand in front of my brothers once they heard about what had transpired?

I assumed Alexander already knew. He was Sadie's best friend after all, and I guarantee he had wormed his way into her business, chalking me up as the villain of this tragic tale.

And so, for better or for worse I left, because that's what I knew best.

I was grateful for the trust fund Mother had left for me. It had gone untouched for years, having no need or access to it while I was serving overseas. But now, it would take care of me while I got my affairs in order. It wasn't much, as she wasn't the wealthy Turner in the family business, Father was, but it was certainly enough I could survive on at least a few months in a hotel while I found a place and my passion in life.

For the past week, I hadn't seen the light of day, save for the rare times I strolled out onto the balcony from my room for a few minutes before retreating inside. I had barely been sober enough to care about what was going on in my life. I'm sure the hotel bar was making a killing off of my misery.

"Room service. How may I direct your call?" a cheery woman answered, after I had dialed the same number I had for seven days.

"Is the bar open yet?" I asked.

The woman paused. "Sir, it's only half-past noon. The bar doesn't open until eight o'clock this evening."

I slapped my forehead and fell back onto the stiff mattress. We went over the same routine every day. I would call as soon as I woke up to see if I could get a bottle of tequila sent to my room, and the lovely lady on the other end would remind me that breakfast was still being served and would ask if I would like anything.

"Right, I must've forgotten," I mumbled. "Sorry, do you think I could have some food sent up to my room? I'm famished."

"Absolutely, feel free to have a look at the menu left in your room and you can give us a call right back when you're ready."

"Alright, I'll do that. Also, do you sell Tylenol downstairs?"

She giggled, making my cheeks flush. "Yes, of course, whatever you need. We'll be more than happy to accommodate. Do you mind if I put you on hold for a second?"

"Sure, no problem," I grunted, applying pressure to my temples, hoping it would alleviate some of the pain in my head.

"Sorry about that," the woman returned. "You have a guest who wishes to speak with you. A Mr. Benjamin Turner. Is it alright if I send him up?"

My heart hammered in my chest. I had no idea how he was able to find me, or what he would even want to talk about. I had been smart and I left my work phone and all other trackable devices back at the mansion. Not to mention we all had different mothers, so there was no way he would be able to know I was using the money she had left to me.

Swallowing a lump in my throat, I nodded, not that she could see. "Yes, that's fine. You can let him up."

"Splendid. Is there anything else I can assist you with at the moment, Mr. Turner?"

"No, that's it for now. I'll call back about the menu, thanks."

Hanging up the landline, I frantically raced around my suite trying to clean up as much as I could. Every day the hotel maid had tried to come in to do some tidying up, but I always shooed her away. I wanted to wallow away in my sorrows. If that meant being surrounded by dirty clothes, empty cups, and takeout containers, so be it.

Luckily, the room had a hamper, so collecting all the clothes was easy, and I poured all the glasses into the kitchen sink and stacked them in the dishwasher. Just as I rounded up the last of the trash, there was a firm knock at the door.

Although I knew who was on the other side, I still looked through the peep hole and confirmed it was indeed, my brother Ben.

Unlocking the door, I whipped it open, and he gave me a once-over from the boots up, shaking his head in disbelief.

"You look awful, dude."

"It's nice to see you too, brother. Remind me again why I should let you in?" I seethed.

"Because I'm pretty much the only family you've got left who isn't trying to ruin your life or who you hate. Besides, I know things."

I cocked an eyebrow, and he crossed his arms over his chest, leaning his weight onto one side.

"Go on," I urged.

"I'm sure you don't want the whole hotel knowing how you royally messed up," Ben muttered.

Groaning, I waved him in, and he scrunched up his nose. I had become adapted to the unpleasant odor of not leaving a room for an entire week, but apparently outsiders were not as accustomed to the stench of alcohol, dirty dishes, and men who had not bathed in days.

I had never allowed any member of the Turner family to see me in such a vulnerable state. I built my walls high enough that none could climb it, but perhaps now was the time to let them in.

"Have you heard from Sadie at all? How is she? What about the girls and her Nana?" Sadie was, and would always be my number one concern and priority.

Benjamin sighed, taking a seat at the two-person eating table in the middle of the kitchen. He remained silent for a few minutes, twirling his thumbs, and I wondered if he was going to speak at all.

"You should sit," he said quietly, motioning toward the other chair.

I did not like where this was going. Gnawing on the inside of my cheek, I slipped into the chair, studying every expression my brother made. I could tell he was trying to work out the words in a gentle manner, but I just wished he would spit it out already.

"I'm not sure how much you were aware of Sadie and Jack's arrangements when he hired her to work for us, but after she had been evicted from her apartment, he had offered her family a place to stay while she was living in the mansion. It was a deal-breaker for her to make sure the twins and her Nana had a roof over their heads."

"And?"

"And, after her employment was terminated, so was their lease on the apartment. He was gracious enough to give her a week to find a new place to live, but she was desperate."

I squeezed my hands into fists and slammed them hard down on the table. "I'm going to kill Jack next time I see him."

"It's not him you have to worry about," Ben muttered. "Guess who swooped in to save the day?"

"Alex."

His name was like poison in my mouth. Of course he did. Sadie always said she would never accept charity, but what choice did she have with only a week and no money? I hated the idea that my brother had something to hold over her head. I just hoped he genuinely cared for her enough that he would never hurt her.

"That's not the worst part."

"There's more?" I wheezed. I wasn't sure how many more revelations I could handle before I stormed the mansion myself and beat them as I did my father.

"Turns out, Chloe's not the best at keeping secrets," Benjamin smirked, leaning back into his chair, and picking at the non-existent dirt from beneath his fingernails. "She just couldn't wait to gloat to Robert about how she and Alex told Wyatt that they had a break-in and needed to check the security footage."

"Who's Robert?"

"My assistant. They were behind Jack finding out about you and Sadie. It's Alex's fault that she's gone."

Cursing every word in the book, I paced back and forth, unable to sit still. I knew in my heart that he had been responsible for our downfall, but never in a million years did I think that he would ever deliberately ruin her life. Sadie had said that this job was the only reason she was going to be able to apply to law school. Without Jack's help, that dream would surely slip through her fingers.

What kind of a best friend was he? Sadie needed to know the truth. But would she believe me, especially after I left her for a second time?

"Who else knows?" I asked.

"Just you. I didn't even tell Jack. I thought I'd come to you first, so we could form an alliance."

"An alliance?" I mused. So, there was a catch, after all. I should have known. It was in Turner blood to cut deals, even with family.

"You and I both know that I'll never be Jack's successor," Ben said. He looked almost defeated at saying so out loud, and I wished I knew how to comfort him. "I'm too soft to run a business like that, but strangely, I'm fine with it. But we cannot let out brother take the lead. I know about the shady warehouse deal. He'll run everything Jack built into the ground if he even gets a taste at ownership. It has to be you."

"I renounced all fealty to Jack and his company; I can't just go back on my hands and knees and beg for his forgiveness."

"Maybe not, but you can prove that you're the better man in every way," Benjamin suggested.

"How do you expect me to do that?"

"In less than two weeks, Jack's hosting a New Year's Eve event and all of the prestige clients and potential clients will be in attendance. It's the perfect place to make your mark, and to show Jack just how much you mean business. But might I suggest cleaning yourself up a bit?"

I looked down at the dirty, wrinkled shirt, and scratched at the stubble of my beard. Luckily, there was plenty of time to take care of such things.

"Why are you helping me now?" I asked.

Benjamin stood up and readjusted his tie before heading for the door. He stopped then, turning slightly, a smile curling at his lips. "Because we're more than just blood. We're brothers, and that's what brothers too. We look out for each other."

Chapter 15:

Nate

"So, what's the occasion?"

The tailor scribbled down my measurements at the local suit shop. I picked out a nice navy-blue material. I wanted to look my best for the New Year's Eve event. I figured every other man in the room would be wearing black and this way, I would stand out from the crowd.

"Business event. I need to look sharp," I stated.

The man nodded. "We'll have this ready by the end of the week. Just make sure you pick it up by Friday, as we're closed for the holidays after that."

"Yes, of course."

I wanted to say that my assistant would be happy to pick it up before the week was out, but I clamped my mouth shut. I did not have an assistant or anyone who was helping me out besides Benjamin, who had come by the hotel a few more times to fill me in on some missing details.

He had tried to get me Sadie's new phone number, but to no surprise, Alex refused to give it up. Apparently, Sadie wanted nothing to do with our family anymore, besides him. He claimed it was his duty as her best friend to protect her at all costs. I wondered if he had hoped they would become more than friends after our falling out. That was the only possible explanation as to why he wanted to keep us apart—it was so he could have her all to himself.

I couldn't help but feel sorry for my brother. He was the jealous type; he was never satisfied with what he had, and he always wanted what I had too. After he had found out that I, in fact, had Sadie first, he had been spiraling ever since. It was only a matter of time before he dug himself so far down that he wouldn't be able to climb out.

I paid the tailor in cash and made a reminder on my phone to pick up the suit by Friday and went on my way. Just as I stepped out of the shop, my phone started ringing, but I did not recognize the number.

Clicking *accept*, I brought the phone to my ear and switched into customer-service mode. "Hello?" I answered.

"Good afternoon. May I please speak with Mr. Nathaniel Turner?" the man asked.

"Speaking. May I ask who's calling?"

"This is Mr. Frank Stockford. I'm a representative of Anthony's Attorney and Law Services. I'm calling on behalf of Jack Turner. It seems you've been involved in an illegal business deal while employed by the company, and now Jack's facing a tremendous lawsuit. You're required to come in and deal with this matter at once or else you may face criminal charges and jail time for up to ten years."

I clutched a hand over my heart and stumbled down the sidewalk for a second before slipping off to the side so I could be out of everyone's path. Resting a hand on the stone wall, I collected myself before speaking.

"I'm sorry, I'm just a little bit confused. Every deal I made with the company was legitimate. You're more than welcome to go through all of my files and see for yourself."

"We have, Mr. Turner. It seems you tried to fly under the radar with this last deal you made before leaving your grandfather's company; however, the deal fell through, and now it's costing Mr. Turner millions to rectify the situation. If you do not come in this afternoon to start handling this dispute, we as his attorneys, will have no choice but to take legal action."

Rage stirred in the pit of my stomach. There was no way that any of the deals Sadie and I made were illegal. No, there had to be some reasonable explanation to prove this was a false accusation. However, the only way to do that was to face Jack and my weasel of a brother. I had pulled out every last file we had in our records office. I would not go down for this.

"Where is this meeting being held?" I asked through gritted teeth.

"The tower. Jack's office. Can you be there within the hour?" Frank asked.

"I'll head there now," I stated. "Is there anything I should know beforehand?"

"I hope you have a really great lawyer, Mr. Turner. You're going to need one."

He hung up at that, and I shoved my phone in my pocket. I was tempted to punch the stone wall, but figured it wouldn't look the best to show up with bloody knuckles. Little did Mr. Stockford know that I had absolutely no connections to any legal representatives, except Sadie Thatcher herself. And there was no chance I was going to drag her into this mess.

It seemed I would have to represent myself and hope that it would be enough.

* * *

Wyatt met me at the front doors of the building.

He was accompanied by three other men, all of whom wore sunglasses, which I thought was oddly unnecessary, considering we were meeting indoors.

"Good afternoon, Wyatt," I said, extending my hand to shake it. "Long time no see."

He frowned, and after side-eyeing his new entourage, shook my hand despite their obvious disapproval. "I'm sorry it has come to this."

"Wyatt, we've been instructed not to engage with Nathaniel without lawyers present," the man with the beard muttered. "I trust Jack would not be pleased with unnecessary pleasantries."

Wyatt placed both hands on his hips and stared the three of them down. "I'll speak to any member of the Turner family how I please. I serve them all, including Nate. Now, if you're done with your whining, let's all go upstairs and join the party. Shall we?"

He waved toward the elevator and the four of us followed behind. Sweat trickled down my spine as we all silently huddled together in the elevator that strangely felt too small. I wasn't one to let my nerves get the better of me, but watching the numbers go up and up, feeling the heavy gaze of these nameless men, my throat suddenly felt itchy and dry. I hoped they would have the decency to at least offer me a glass of water when I got up there.

The elevator bell dinged, the doors opened, and we all filed out one by one. I knew the floor off by heart, but still, they flanked me as I made my way to my grandfather's office. I swore they were muttering things to each other, but I couldn't quite make out the words. Before all of this, I would have demanded they speak up, but I knew that now was not the time or place for aggressive behavior.

No, I had to play pretend to get through this, even if it went against my fundamental nature.

"Right this way," the bearded man said.

"I'm quite familiar with the whereabouts of Jack's office, thank you," I grumbled, unable to stop myself.

Wyatt smirked, but did not say a word.

Waltzing into his office, I spotted Jack immediately, who remained seated in his huge leather chair behind his mahogany desk. Only the best for my grandfather. On his left, was an older man, probably old enough to be my father, who wore a red suit and had dark skin. I could only assume this was Frank, the man I spoke with on the phone. Wyatt's posse remained outside the office, but stood like big, strong men with their arms crossed over their chests. I rolled my eyes in disgust. They had no idea what it meant to be a strong man. I'm sure Mateo would agree that a few years of service would straighten them out. Wyatt stayed by the door, ready to obey any command that Jack might have, as his assistant was nowhere to be seen.

There was only a single chair placed opposite to them. I had hoped that perhaps they would have called Sadie to ask for her statement and I would get to see her again. A frivolous thought at best; I wouldn't want her to have to sit through all this male ego strutting anyway. She was better off staying as far away from the Turner brothers as possible.

"Nathaniel Turner, please have a seat and we'll get started."

"I think I'd like to stand," I challenged, shoving my hands into my pants pockets, staring daggers into Frank's eyes.

"Nate," Jack growled. "Now's not the time to see who's the king of the castle. Sit your ass in that chair so we can fix what we can of your mess."

"Fine, show me this supposed illegal business deal I made so I can prove to you all that it's incorrect and we can all go about our days."

Frank huffed and proceeded to dive into his briefcase. He muttered under his breath until he retrieved what he was looking for. "Before we begin, you'll address all questions and comments to me. I'm representing Jack Turner; he does not need to speak, only sit in as a witness to our conversation."

"Whatever you say, Mr. Stockford."

"Alright, let's begin. First, will you please confirm that this is you in this picture alongside Miss Sadie Thatcher?"

He pulled out a large photograph. Sadie wore a short black dress and sparkly high heels. I remembered the night all too well. It was when I caught that wretched man sucking on her face as if his life depended on it. I also recalled I had tracked her work phone to some sketchy warehouse that Alex had supposedly turned into a nightclub.

"Yes, that's us," I stated. My arm was wrapped around her shoulder and the image had been captured of us just leaving the club. Just out of view, was my vehicle. For a second, my mind flashed to our kiss, and me telling her I did not want her kissing any other boys.

"So, you're admitting that you've been to The Crypt before?" Frank said. I knew he was jumping to conclusions, and I quickly pieced together what he was trying to get me to confess. The shady warehouse deal—that's what all of this was about.

"The Crypt?" I laughed, shoving the photograph back across the table. "Once. I went there to retrieve my assistant, Miss Thatcher, who was brought there, not knowing that it was an underground establishment."

The last thing I needed was to get Sadie charged too, just for being there.

"An underground establishment that you purchased without Jack's consent," Frank explained. He rifled through more papers and presented them in front of me. There were contracts, deeds, and agreements, all signed with my name.

Mr. Nathaniel Turner.

"I've never seen these before in my life," I breathed. For the first time, I did not have any snide remarks.

"Funny, that's your name signed at the bottom of every page," Frank continued. "And again, on authorized checks from Jack's business. As it turns out, The Crypt's location was seized by the bank months ago and wasn't available for purchase. Whoever you bought it from was just looking for some easy cash, and you fell right into his trap."

No, I wanted to say, *my stupid brother did.*

"I'm telling you; this is all one huge misunderstanding, I did not sign any of these, nor did I take any of Jack's money—"

"You have exactly thirty days to come up with the money or we'll have to take this to court. Jack is being generous with this offer. I, on the other hand, suggested you be apprehended immediately. However, it's his decision."

"Jack, you know I would never do this to you. It's Alex. He's the one who purchased the club, not me. Look at the dates, I bet some of them go as far back as when I was still overseas."

"That'll be all, Mr. Turner," Frank snapped. He stood up and with a snap of his fingers, the security guards jumped into action. "My associates will see you out."

There was so much more I wanted to say to my grandfather, to try and convince him that my brother could not be trusted, but what could I do? All the evidence pointed to me. Now it seemed like our little New Year's Eve plan was slipping through my fingers too.

Chapter 16:

Sadie

"Hey Sadie, do you mind running down the street and getting us all coffee? I forgot to stop on my way in."

My new boss, Mr. Davis, poked his head around the corner, flashing me a toothy smile. I had been working as his new office assistant for two weeks now, and so far, things were going well. Luckily, I had gone to school a few years ago and received a diploma, so I was able to work as a legal assistant. It was definitely one up from working at a coffee shop and hostess at a restaurant. The pay was great, and although I had to put my dreams of becoming a lawyer on hold, perhaps if I stayed on with them for a few years, they might sponsor my tuition in the long run. It was all about playing the waiting game.

"Absolutely, Mr. Davis. I'd be more than happy to do that for you."

"Also, this just came expedited for you," he said, handing me a large FedEx envelope. "I had to sign for it, but it says it came from one of our sister branches. Are you doing some sleuthing I should be aware of?" He gave me a playful look, but I waved my hand nonchalantly.

"Nothing you need to concern yourself with. Just looking into a cold case for a friend, that's all."

"You'll make a great lawyer someday, kid." He gave my shoulder a quick squeeze before disappearing down the hallway, leaving the corporate credit card in his place.

Knowing that the contents of the envelope could quite possibly contain some life-altering information, I thought it was best to run to the coffee shop before I found the courage to see what was inside.

Twenty minutes later, I settled back into my desk at the front of the office, sinking as far down into my chair as possible so I could use the top of the desk as a sort of shield from the outside world. Our office was on the main level of the building, and with massive glass windows and doors, I could sit and people-watch all day long. But now was not the time to get distracted. Ripping the seal off the envelope, I dug out two separate files, but opened the one with Adam Turner's name on it first.

Skipping the pages, my heart sank into my stomach, piecing together all the clues of Nate's mother's accident. It was all here—how had no one convicted his father sooner? How was this man walking free? Not only were there traces of his DNA in the vehicle that his mother was driving, but in the one that had crashed into hers as well. That meant it was preplanned. He must have paid someone off somewhere down the line to make this disappear. But you couldn't erase everything; these files were proof of that. Even if Nate did not deserve my love or forgiveness, I couldn't just sweep something like this under the rug. I wouldn't be able to sleep at night.

Adam Turner would get what he deserved. I would make sure of that.

The second file was far less dramatic. Mr. Gabriel Perez, born and raised in the city, worked as a banker down on Fourth Street. All this time, he was right under my nose and I had no idea. Taking in a deep breath, I used the work phone to dial the last known number on file for him and waited.

It rang three times before a man's voice answered.

"Hello?"

"Hi," I said, clearing my throat. "Is this Gabriel Perez?"

"Speaking. How can I help you?"

"My name is Sadie Thatcher. I believe you knew my mother. I— I don't really know how to tell you this, but I think you're my dad."

* * *

My legs bobbed up and down as I waited patiently for Gabriel to arrive.

After dropping the bomb on him that I believed he was my father, he was more than enthused to meet me. We agreed to go somewhere mutual so that neither one of us would feel uncomfortable or ambushed. I chose a quiet little restaurant just on the outside of town that had a wonderful outdoor patio. He said he would be there by seven o'clock.

I hadn't told Nana where I was going when I got home. I just told her that she should not wait up for me, and after kissing the twins goodbye, I hopped into an Uber and made my way to the restaurant.

Right at seven o'clock, a man with short black hair and my skin tone pulled up in a Mercedes Benz. I felt a bit overdressed, since I did not have the time to change out of my work clothes, and he was in a button-down shirt with jeans. He walked up to the hostess, who pointed in my direction. I wasn't sure if I should sit or stand, so I remained glued to my seat.

"Sadie?" Gabriel asked as he approached, a plastic menu in hand. "Are you Sadie?"

"Yes," I breathed. "You must be Gabriel."

"That's right." He pulled out one of the red metal chairs at my table and took a seat. I noticed he had a few photos sticking out of the pocket of his shirt, and he caught me staring. "I brought these. It took me a while to fish them out of my storage unit, but I thought you'd want to see them."

He handed them over and it was further confirmation that this man was indeed my dad. My mother looked young and happy, just like the pictures Nana had around the house. I brushed my fingertips on them, tears burning my eyes. They fell, and I quickly wiped them off the photographs, not wanting to ruin them.

"She's beautiful," I said, my voice cracking ever so slightly. "She looks like Nana."

"Her mother?" Gabriel asked.

"Yes, she lives with me. I never met my mother." I offered back the photographs, but he shook his head, waving for me to hold onto them.

"Did she, uh, pass when you were young?"

I could tell he wasn't exactly sure how he should broach the subject, but I wasn't a child who needed coddling. I was a grown woman with two young girls of my own.

"No," I said harshly. "She dumped me off on my Nana's porch shortly after she gave birth to me. She left a note saying she did not have what it took to be a mother, and that she was born to be free. We never heard from her since. It was Nana who raised me, so she's the only mother I've ever known. I suspect she never told you about me."

Gabriel shook his head, and I swore I saw tears forming in his eyes. "I wish she had. I would've been there for you, even though we were young. I would've been the father you needed, Sadie."

He reached over and grabbed my hand and gave it a gentle squeeze. I closed my eyes for a second, allowing the tears to fall, before using the back of my sleeve to dry my face. "And a grandfather," I murmured, showing him the lock screen of my phone.

He gasped, taking it gingerly, staring at the picture of Nora and Sarah for what felt like an hour. "They're precious."

"That one's Nora and the other is Sarah. Twins," I giggled, "I too had them when I was young."

"And their father? Please tell me they had it better than you did."

I sighed, placing the phone down on the table. "I'm afraid he left before I even found out that I was pregnant."

"Aw, that's terrible," Gabriel said. "I'm so sorry."

"It's not your fault, none of this is. I'm nearly thirty, and it's taken me this long to try and track you down. I guess I was just afraid of what I would find if you did know about me and didn't want anything to do with me."

"So, what changed your mind?"

I hesitated for a minute, unsure if I wanted to go down this path—to admit that I had made a choice to keep my kids from their dad after he had come back into our lives. I did not want Gabriel to think I was a coward.

"Well, the truth is, their father and I crossed paths again. Just a few months ago. I worked for him. It's really rather ironic. Perhaps the stars had aligned for us once more. Or so I had thought. But, when reality hit and life tried to tear us apart again, he made it easy for the universe to sever our ties. He left again, just like he did the first time. I never even told him about the girls. He has no idea that he's a dad."

"I see," Gabriel murmured. "You want to protect them. There's nothing wrong with that."

"Am I protecting them, though?" My chin trembled, and I was on the verge of tears again. "I can say with my whole heart that I would've rather had met you, even if it was only once than to have never known my father at all."

"If I may be so bold to say, but it sounds like you're looking for my permission to tell this man that they're his kids."

"I don't know what I want," I admitted. "All I know is, there's a hole in my heart because I grew up not knowing either one of my parents. Nana told me stories of my mom of course, back when she was a kid and a teenager. She said she used to be so full of love and life, she never understood why she'd ever want to give me up. Unfortunately, she knew very little about you—just a name that my mother had mentioned in passing. Then, nine months later, I popped out."

"Mary was a brilliant, strong woman, even at that age. She'd be the center of attention no matter where she went, even without trying. She wanted so much, had such big ambitions."

"A baby would've held her back," I whispered.

He stopped, and it was clear my thought was right. I knew it as much, even if I never wanted to think about it. I could never imagine being apart from Nora and Sarah. They were my whole life—the reason I get up every morning and face the world, regardless of the hurdles I have had to overcome. They give me strength when I need it most.

"Whatever her reason, I'm grateful to have met her, because if not, you would not exist. And I'd love to get to know you more, and perhaps down the road, meet those sweet little girls of yours."

"I'd love that," I smiled. "I'm sure they would, too."

Chapter 17:

Nate

"Are you sure you want to do this, sir?"

Lydia, my new assistant, sat in the passenger seat as we slowly drove through the chaotic streets of downtown. It was New Year's Eve, and everything was packed—bars, restaurants, even the streets were swarming with pedestrians. It was odd to have another woman sit in the seat that Sadie had occupied so many times, but I tried not to dwell on it. I couldn't do this alone—not after the warehouse incident—and there was only so much Ben and Robert could do from their end. Besides, this wasn't their fight; it was mine.

"Yes," I said, not taking my eyes off the road, even if we were barely crawling through traffic. "Besides, if I know my brother, he won't even be there yet. He'll arrive fashionably late as usual, and drunk as a skunk."

Lydia snorted. I gave her a sideways glance only to see her scrolling through her phone, jumping from app to app. She was young, barely an adult by my standards, but she was fresh blood and not my ex-girlfriend, so she had that much going for her. She had come recommended by Benjamin, who assured me she would be able to handle whatever I threw at her. So far, she had lived up to those expectations, even if she wasn't much of a conversationalist. It was a quality I liked, since I wasn't either.

"Alright, and what about Jack? He does have a pending lawsuit against you. I'm sure he won't appreciate you crashing his party, especially with so many people watching."

"You printed everything I emailed you?" I asked.

She patted the black briefcase in her lap. "All here."

"Then he won't be an issue. Plus, Jack isn't one to make a scene. He'll stay quiet until we're no longer in public."

"You hope," she reiterated. "We've got a lot riding on what you think your family members are going to do. This could all come crashing down if they don't even let us in the front door."

Lydia lacked faith in my charm. Perhaps because she had never seen it in action before. But she was about to. "We're almost there. Get your game face on," I smirked, pulling into the parking lot of the country club.

From what Benjamin had told me, it was where Jack held his New Year's Eve party every year. Not that I had ever attended one myself. I expected it to be nothing short of extravagant and expensive. Anything to impress a potential client.

Fear made its way into my heart when we pulled up to the front entrance and a man was taking down people's names before letting them in. I hadn't thought of that little hurdle, and I doubted that Jack would have me on the guest list.

Before I could come up with any sort of backup plan, the man working valet opened my door and offered to park my car for me. We stepped out, Lydia looking wonderful in her sparkly champagne-colored gown, and me, in my navy blue suit. We looked like we belonged, and I prayed that was enough.

"Be gentle with it," I said, handing him the keys before he slipped into the passenger seat. "Shall we?"

Lydia took my arm and we walked up the steps, where the man stationed at the podium ordered us to halt. "Names?"

"Nathaniel Turner and guest," I said.

He flipped through the pages trying to find my name somewhere, but as expected, it wasn't there. "I'm sorry sir. Are you sure you received an invitation?"

"He's clear," a voice said.

I looked up to find Wyatt looming over the man's shoulder. His glare had the ability to intimidate any weak man, but I was not one of them. With a rushed wave of his hands, he let us through, and Lydia couldn't help but smirk in my direction.

"Nicely played." She winked at Wyatt.

"And who might you be?"

"A family friend," I responded. "Thanks, I appreciate it."

"Just try and stay out of trouble," Wyatt whispered.

"Has Alex arrived yet?"

"No. I suspect he'll be here within the hour though."

Perfect. That gave us lots of time to execute our plan. "And Benjamin?"

"Already inside. I know that look—I suggest you better get a move on with whatever plans you've got up your sleeve."

"Redemption. That's what I have planned. And I don't plan on leaving without it."

As Wyatt bid us both good luck, Lydia and I made our way to the event room. There was no need for signs, as the sound of voices and music was loud enough to act as our guide. The double doors were left open, and upon entering, I was overwhelmed by the number of people and couples in attendance. Benjamin never said Jack catered to the entire city. There had to be close to five hundred people there including the mayor, city governors, wealthy businessmen who I had made deals with during my short time working for my grandfather. Luckily, I hadn't seen the man himself yet, which I hoped meant he hadn't seen me.

"Mr. Turner!"

I whirled around to see Mr. Richards walking toward me. I remembered him instantly—the tailored suit and massive rings he wore on each of his fingers. He was one of the first major sales Alex and I made with Jack.

"Mr. Richards," I greeted, shaking his hand. "What a pleasant surprise. How are you?"

"I'm well, thanks to you and your grandfather." He winked. "And who is this beautiful young woman?"

"Lydia," she said, smiling sweetly. "I'm Mr. Turner's new assistant."

"What happened to the other one?" he said, his face scrunching in confusion. "I quite liked her."

"She had another opportunity come up," I lied. "I wouldn't let her pass on it."

"You're a good man," Mr. Richards declared. "Come, let me introduce you to some of my friends."

Half an hour flew by and I became the man to meet. I had shaken so many hands that I lost count. Men clinked their glasses with mine, and ladies blushed as I looked into their eyes. I even spotted Mateo, my former military commander, in the crowd. I hadn't even had the chance to go over and greet him as I was swarmed by the clientele. To top it all off, Jack had walked by several times, and I could have sworn his eyes were beaming with approval. Perhaps I was not out of the race just yet.

However, just as everything seemed to be falling into place, my dearest brother had to set it all ablaze.

"What in the hell are you doing here?" he hissed.

It was as if the entire room heard his shrill little voice, as the crowd hushed to watch our little spectacle.

My lip curled into a sly grin. Alex was always so predictable. He made it all too easy to be taken advantage of.

"What does it look like? I'm mingling, I suggest you do the same. Perhaps give other people a chance to go to the bar."

Several men chuckled at my joke, and some even dared to point and laugh at his expense. His face turned beet red, not just because he clearly had one too many drinks, but from the utter embarrassment of being made to look like a fool.

"You are not welcome here," he continued. "This party is for Jack's closest friends and family. You gave up every right to be here when you made a mockery of the Turner name."

"Did I?" I tilted my head to the side, letting my question linger between us. I wanted to cherish the moment when Alex would finally get what he deserved. "From the way I see it, it was you who forged my signature on all those documents. It was you who stole our grandfather's money so you could run an illegal nightclub and leech off the profits. Lydia—" I looked around the room for my assistant, and was pleased she had only been standing a few steps away. "Will you please show him the evidence you collected?"

She smiled and handed him the huge stack of papers from her soft briefcase. "We even have over fifty witnesses who have all agreed to stand beside Nate's claim that you were the one who bought The Crypt, not him."

Right on schedule, Jack stepped in to intervene. "What is the meaning of this?" he demanded.

"I'm just showing you Alex's true colors, that's all. And clearing my name in the process."

"Let me see those." He snapped his fingers at Alex, forcing him to hand the incriminating evidence over.

"Jack, please, I can explain—"

"Silence," he hissed. "You are a complete and utter disgrace. Friends, family, if you could gather around, I have an announcement to make."

No one moved, as they had already corralled themselves as close to us as possible to watch Alex's whole life unravel before his very eyes. All I could do was smile as he crumbled to nothing.

"As you know, there's been talk about me stepping down as CEO of the company that has brought us all together tonight. I'm here to tell you that those rumors are true. I'm getting old now, and for the past few weeks, it's been my life's mission to find a successor worthy of taking my place. I'd narrowed it down to my three grandsons; Benjamin, Alexander, and Nathaniel. I certainly did not make things easy for them, because I wanted to make sure my legacy would be left in great hands. Well, it brings me great pleasure to officially announce who will be taking my place. Let's all give a warm welcome to Nathaniel Turner, your new CEO!"

The crowd clapped and cheered, and Lydia gave me a congratulatory hug, even though I desperately wished she were someone else at this moment. I watched Alex storm off like a child who had just been told they couldn't be the leader of the group.

"Jack, I don't know what to say," I mumbled.

"You've earned it, but don't make me regret my decision," he chuckled. "Enjoy this moment. They don't come along very often."

"Well done, Nate." Mateo appeared out of nowhere, slapping an open hand on my back. "You're a lucky man."

The rest of the night became a blur of champagne, handshakes, and congratulations.

Chapter 18:

Sadie

"Yeah, we're right around the corner from Adam's Auto Repairs. Yeah, Sadie's with me, she brought the paperwork to hand over to the cops once we get there."

Mr. Davis had agreed to accompany me to Adam's arrest. I told him that he did not need to go out of his way, that I would be fine to do this on my own, but he insisted. Secretly, I was grateful for it. I had never had the pleasure of meeting Nate's dad before, and I was certain he was not going to like me after this. I did not care though. His mother needed justice, and that was the most important thing.

"We're here," he said.

My heart fluttered in my chest. I recognized the SUV parked out front of the shop and knew things were about to bet ten times worse, but there was no turning back now. Several cop cars pulled in after us with their sirens blaring and lights flashing.

In a matter of seconds, a man who looked kind of like Nate stormed out of the building. He was dressed in a blue uniform that was covered in grease, as were his hands and arms. Smudges of dirt were caked on his face, and his eyes were red and filled with anger.

"What's the meaning of this?" he shouted as several cops walked toward him.

"Adam Turner, you're under arrest for your involvement in the murder of Lauren Pierce. You have the right to remain silent. Anything you say can be used against you in court." The chief proceeded with the rest of the Miranda rights, as he cuffed Adam's hands behind his back.

"Please, you don't understand. I had nothing to do with—"

"Shut up," one of the female cops snapped. "You were read your rights. We already have evidence that ties you to the car that crashed into Lauren's. You're going away for life."

Adam's pleas shook me to my very core, and I couldn't stop my tears as I watched him get hauled into the back of a police car.

"You must be Miss Thatcher," the chief of police said. "I believe you have some paperwork for me?"

"Yes," I said, looking at Mr. Davis for a second before handing over the extensive file. "It's all in there."

"You'd be a great detective," he said, giving us a short bow and leaving with the rest of the team.

"And an amazing lawyer," Mr. Davis bumped shoulders with me.

At that, Alex came barreling out of the auto shop shouting at the top of his lungs. "What are you doing? My father is innocent!"

There was no one around willing to listen to his screams. The cops who stayed behind paid him no attention, so he turned to look at me. Hot, angry tears streamed down his face, and I could have sworn that he looked like he wanted to rip me to shreds. Mr. Davis must have noticed it too, as he used his body to block me from his path.

"You— How could you do this to him?" Alex cried.

"He was involved in Nate's mother's murder," I explained. "I couldn't just let him get away with it."

"That man was my last hope of survival!" Alex shrieked. "Without him, I have nothing left."

"What are you talking about?"

"Oh, playing dumb, are we? Are you trying to tell me Nate hasn't tracked you down to gloat about his new position as CEO of the company?"

"Nate's still in town? I thought you said he left?"

None of this made sense. Why would Alex lie about something like that? Especially when he knew how heartbroken I was that Nate had left me behind for a second time.

"When are you going to grow up, Sadie?" Alex shook his head, laughing as if this was a comical situation.

165

"Nate didn't go anywhere, and he's been trying to get a hold of you ever since you left the mansion."

Tears burned my eyes at hearing his confession. "I don't understand. You're telling me you deliberately kept us apart. Even though you knew I loved him?"

"That's why I did it!" he shouted, spit flying from his mouth. "He doesn't deserve you, Sade. No one does!"

"Except you," I seethed. "Right?"

That stopped him in his tracks. After everything we had been through in the past ten years, I had blindly accepted every word he said as the truth. He had watched me raise the girls, was a part of every aspect of their life, attended every birthday, every holiday, and showered them with gifts whenever possible. And for what? To try to win my heart?

"Why can't you love me the same way you do him? You know I'd never leave you. I've been here all along."

"As my best friend!" I yelled. "I didn't realize everything you'd done had strings attached."

"I love you, Sadie. Please tell me you love me."

"I can't. I'm sorry." Mr. Davis tugged on my elbow, grounding me in this awful reality. "I have to go."

"Sadie, wait. Please don't do this. Don't leave."

"Goodbye, Alex."

***

It had been a little over a week since Adam's arrest.

The chief of police assigned to his case said it was a no-brainer—that Nate's dad was going away for a very long time. After everything that had transpired that day, at least there was some light in the sea of darkness. I wasn't sure if my heart would ever be whole again after Alex's betrayal. After days apart, I had found clarity in the dynamic of our friendship. He thought that money and possessions would somehow buy my love. I wasn't sure if it had always been that way, or if Nate's return and our relationship brought it on. Either way, I did not care to know. Things would never be the same between us again.

Which meant that I would have to pick my family up and move, for what felt like the hundredth time in the past six months.

All I wanted was something permanent in my life, so the girls wouldn't have to keep packing up their things and moving to a new place every few weeks. Unfortunately, life did not come with an instruction manual, and I had to do the best I could with what I had.

Mr. Davis offered me some comfort in the fact that he waived my probation period, so I would never have to worry about losing my job for no reason. Plus, the pay was good, so I could afford rent, groceries, bills, and still have some leftover for savings. It wasn't much, but it was enough to survive, and we would all stay together.

Gabriel even offered to help us move, which I thought would be a great opportunity for him to be able to bond with his grandchildren.

Sitting on my bedroom floor, I started taking things out of my closet, one by one, and piling them on the bed. I wanted to make sure we were out of Alex's apartment as soon as possible. I did not think he would ever do anything rash with the girls around, but I wasn't going to risk it. Besides, it was about time I cut ties with him once and for all.

Grabbing an old shoebox, my heart skipped a beat after catching a glimpse at what was written on the side.

High school memories.

Biting my bottom lip, I slipped down the wall and held the box in my hands before removing the lid. Pictures of Nate and I sat on top, and I clutched them to my heart, allowing silent tears to fall down my cheeks. I flipped through them slowly. In some of the photos, we were with our group of friends, and in others just the two of us at the beach, the movies, the carnival, or in class. He was my first real love and after our reunion, a part of me hoped he had be my last. No one ever compared to Nate Turner, and I knew no one ever would. Not even if I spent my entire life searching for the perfect man.

Underneath the pictures, I discovered other little mementos that I had hidden away like ultrasound images from when I found out I was pregnant with the twins. I remembered that day as if it were yesterday. It had been less than a month after Nate's mysterious disappearance. I had missed a period, and while that wasn't usual, all the other little symptoms had me worried. After taking a pregnancy test and seeing those two pink lines, my whole world was changed forever.

At the time, I thought my life was over before it even started. But that wasn't the case. Nora and Sarah were a gift—they were little pieces of Nate and me.

Pressing a hand to my stomach, I smiled knowing that the third would bring me just as much joy as the first two did. Maybe, just maybe, the father would get a chance to see them grow up. I had hope that he would.

"Sadie," Nana called out. "There's a letter here for you from Harvard University."

I scrambled out of the room, bumping into the walls as I nearly crashed into the old woman to get my hands on the envelope. Nearly ripping the contents in two, I scanned the first few sentences, but stopped after reading *Congratulations, we would like to offer you admission next fall.*

"So, what does it say?" Nana squealed.

"I've been accepted into the program," I said, falling into a chair. "I can't believe it."

"Oh darling, I'm so proud of you!" She squeezed me tight and gave me a big kiss on the forehead.

"Yeah, it's just an honor to be accepted. It's too bad that I won't be able to attend," I mumbled. "I should probably give them a call and let them know I don't have the funds."

"Even with this new job?" Nana asked, her eyes glistening with tears.

"Afraid not," I sighed.

Taking the acceptance letter with me, I disappeared down the hallway and closed my bedroom door so I could have some privacy. The financial aid number was conveniently printed at the bottom of the page, so I dialed it and waited patiently.

"Harvard Financial Aid Office. How may I direct your call?"

"Hi. This is Sadie Thatcher calling. I just received an offer of admission, but I sadly have to decline."

"Oh dear," the woman said. "May I ask why?"

"Unfortunately, I won't have the money to pay the tuition fee."

"That's odd," she replied.

"What's odd?"

"It says here in the computer that your tuition has been paid in full, as of a few days ago."

"It has?" I gasped. "Does it say by who?"

"A Mr. Jack Turner. Oh wait, there's a note here attached. It says, *good luck Miss Thatcher. I know you're going to do great things. Love, Jack.* That's so sweet. Is he a relative?"

"Yes." I smiled. "Yes, he is."

Chapter 19:

Nate

Although I had told myself I would never step foot in the mansion again, that turned out to be a lie.

Well, not a lie. More like a bit of an exaggeration. Things were different now. I was different. I felt like a new man in the blink of an eye. One day I was drowning in sorrows and tequila, and the next I was the proud owner of a property investment corporation. I had so many plans for the near future, potential lots to purchase, clients I would love to work with. The past week or so, I had only slept and worked. Lydia never complained, although I knew she was feeling the burnout of working seven days in a row.

While the thought was still in my head, I scribbled down a note to remind myself to give her a paid holiday soon. She deserved it after helping me to get my life back in order. I did not know much about her, but I did know that she and her boyfriend were saving up to buy a house. That explained why she was a bit of a workaholic.

I had tried to make it so neither of us worked on weekends, but I had a lot of stuff to get in order for the transition of CEOs. It was more than just signing a few documents here and there.

Dialing Lydia's work phone, she picked up on the first ring. "Hey, Nate. What's up?"

"I'm so sorry to bother you. I just wanted to double-check with you my meeting schedule for Monday. I seem to have erased it here on my iPad and I don't want to miss anything important."

"Sure. Just give me one second."

I heard a few clicks of her nails typing on the phone until she brought it back to her ear. "You have two appointments booked; one is with Mr. Richards again at nine o'clock in the morning, and the second is with your former commanding officer, Mateo. It says here in the notes that he's looking to buy land for a hunting camp."

"Perfect. Thanks so much."

"Also, Jack just called and said he wants to speak with you."

"Right now?"

"It sounded important."

"Alright. Did he say where?"

"His home office, I believe."

"Sounds good. Thanks so much. I'll chat with you on Monday."

Closing everything down in my office at the mansion, I headed downstairs where I figured I would find Jack. Even though he was passing over the company to me, he was still working. I did not know how he did it. A part of me hoped my life would not be completely consumed with work. I wanted to settle down, have a family, and find the perfect girl to spend the rest of my life with. It hurt my heart knowing that she existed, we had met, and I let her slip through my fingers.

Giving the door a quick knock, I let myself in.

"Hey, Sadie—I mean—Lydia said you wanted to talk."

Jack looked up from his desk and there was something different about him. He looked like he was the one who could use a vacation. His skin was paler than usual, and his eyes looked tired and no longer had a sparkle. I instantly worried that something had happened.

"What's the matter?"

"Sit. Have a drink with your grandpa," he offered. There was a short glass with golden liquid in it. From where I was standing, I could smell it was tequila.

"What's the special occasion?" I asked, taking a seat in one of the leather chairs across from him. I couldn't help but think back to the last time I sat in this position, with Sadie by my side, crying softly into his handkerchief.

"The lawyers finally sent over the paperwork. It's official, you're the CEO."

"That's amazing," I breathed, feeling a weight lift from my shoulders. I knew it was going to happen eventually, but the finality of it all made me feel all warm inside. For the first time in a long time, it felt like I had done something right.

"I have something else to confess," Jack admitted.

"What is it?"

"As you know, I'm getting old, but that's not the only reason that I've decided to retire."

"It's not?"

My mind reeled with all the other possibilities that he could say. His wife had died long ago. Was it possible he met someone else? Did he want to settle down and live the rest of his life in peace, not chasing after buyers and making deals with clients?

"I'm sick, Nate."

I had just brought the glass to my lips, and the smell of alcohol burned my nostrils. My hand hovered there for a few seconds before I brought it down onto the table, leaving it untouched.

"What did you say?"

"I'm sick."

"As in—"

"Cancer. Terminal. There's no cure or treatment that will extend my life any longer than what He has intended."

"I don't understand," I mumbled. "What— How— Why are you just telling me now?"

"I wanted to make sure everything I had built was secure first. That's why I've been gone most days. Doctor's appointment after doctor's appointment, trying to see if there was anything that I could do to buy more time, just in case one of you boys didn't have what it took to stand up to the plate. Your little show at the New Year's Eve event sealed the deal though. I had always known it would be you."

Tears pricked my eyes and I had to swallow hard to regain some sense of composure. What did he expect me to do with this news? How was I going to continue on with my life? Act as if he did not tell me? Start planning his funeral?

"Do you know how much time you have left?" I whispered. I was afraid to even know.

Jack sighed. "Less than six months I would say, if that. I can already feel it. My bones ache when I walk, I'm tired more often, and my appetite is slowly slipping away. I'm dying, to put it plainly, but I don't want you to worry about that. I've already made all the arrangements."

"I don't know what I'm going to do without you," I began. "You've been like a father to me. More than that wretched man ever was. It was you who taught us how to be men; how to drive, how to hunt, and how to make a deal."

"Sadly, we don't get to choose our parents, but you're old enough now that you should know the truth. Adam was a bad man. I'm ashamed to call him my son. Recently, he was arrested for—"

"I already know," I blurted, cutting my grandfather off. "Sadie and I had started working on the investigation when she first arrived at the mansion. Benjamin forwarded me all the documents a few days ago. He's been arrested for the murder of my mother. Well, the part he played."

"I'm so sorry, Nate. No child deserves to grow up without a parent, let alone both."

"Sadie did, and she turned out fine," I said under my breath.

"I'm sorry about that, too. I should've never let her go. I regret that decision, but unfortunately, there's nothing I can do to change the past."

Jack stood up from his desk and went over to the window. Sunlight poured into his office, and in the light, he almost looked like his old self again. But there was nothing I could do to pretend that things would go back to the way they were.

"Do you remember that large sum I took out of the account the other day?" he asked.

"Yeah. You said it was to invest in something. I just can't remember what."

"It was to invest in your future. Her future. I had Wyatt do a little investigating himself and when he caught wind that Sadie had been accepted to Harvard, well, I paid her tuition so she could have a fresh start."

"You did what?"

I could hardly believe my ears. The man who had dismissed her so coldly only weeks prior was now telling me that he had spent thousands of dollars on the tuition for a woman who had only worked for the company for a short period of time.

"She's your soulmate, Nate. You cannot deny it. I saw the way you two looked at each other. It was the same way I looked at your grandma, and she at me. It broke my heart the day I lost her. I had a lot of regrets after that. Time wasted sitting here in this office was time that I could've been with her. If I had known that day would've been her last, I would've cherished every second I had left."

"Why are you telling me all this?"

I could feel the tears starting to form in my eyes again, but I wanted to be strong. If not for me, for him.

"Don't make the same mistakes I did, Nate. I know I've made you believe that work should be your priority, but it isn't everything. Love is. Don't give up, and don't stop fighting. It's the most precious thing in this world, and when it's gone..." He paused, walked over to me, and placed a gentle hand on my shoulder. "You'll feel the empty void left behind."

"I'm afraid it might be too late for us," I admitted.

"Nonsense," Jack wheezed. "You kids are young. It'll only be too late if she's dead. And don't you dare let it come to that." He shook his index finger wildly at me, and I was reminded of his constant scolding throughout my childhood. "Now go. I never said it was going to be easy, and I suspect you'll have a lot of making up to do for running off in the middle of the night instead of facing your problems like a man."

I stood up, a rush of adrenaline pumping through my veins. Perhaps he was right—Sadie was my soulmate, and there was no way I was going to let her go for a third time. Not if I could help it.

"Thanks, Jack."

"Call me Pops. And you better give me a great-grandchild before my time is up. I'll need something to tell your grandma when she and I are reunited."

Chapter 20:

Sadie

"Mr. Davis, I have those documents you wanted."

"Come on in, Sadie!"

Opening the frosted-glass door, I walked over and plopped the pile of files into the tray on the edge of his desk. There were a few in the outgoing stack, so I scooped those up to take care of when I went back to the front desk.

"Is there anything else you need from me? I know you said you were planning on leaving early since it's Friday and all."

"No, I think what you've got in your hands there is everything. I'm just going through my inbox and responding to some last-minute emails and then I'll be out. You have your key?"

"Yes, sir."

I patted my cardigan pocket for good measure before heading back to my area. It was quiet, as all the other lawyers had left for the weekend and it was just Mr. Davis and I. Sometimes he reminded me a bit of Jack in the sense that he liked to work both day and night. It made my heart ache just thinking about the Turner family. I hadn't found the courage to call Jack to thank him for his generosity in paying for my tuition to Harvard this fall. There were so many times that I had picked up the phone and pressed his number, but not once had I actually made the call. I guessed a part of me was just embarrassed by the fact that I had broken the employee contract by engaging in sexual relations with his grandson. It did not matter that we had a history together; a rule was a rule. I broke that because I couldn't control my lust.

The desk phone rang, which was unusual for this time of day. I thought I recognized the number, but then again, I saw so many, it was probably just a coincidence.

"Mr. Davis's office. Sadie speaking. How may I help you?"

"Hello, Sadie. This is Lydia calling on behalf of Mr. Turner. How are you?"

"I'm great. When you say Mr. Turner, do you mean—"

"Nathaniel Turner."

"Oh."

I was tempted to hang up the phone and pretend like I never answered it, but knew that this Lydia woman would likely go crawling to Nate and tell her that I rudely ended the call. Swallowing what was left of my pride, I lifted my chin and put on my bravest face.

"Yeah. I'm so sorry to bother you at work. I know how busy you are, but there do seem to be a few last-minute legal documents here that we need you to sign. I must've forgotten to flag them, but they do need to be dealt with immediately, so I was hoping you'd be able to save my butt and stop by to sign them."

"Legal documents?" I questioned. "I was terminated. I'm not sure what other things there would be for me to sign."

"Uh, it's just a non-disclosure agreement and a few other things. Nothing major, but we do need to handle it on our end as we need records of it."

"And it can't wait until next week?"

Another pause. "Afraid not. We're just getting ready to close the office so is there a chance that you can stop by the mansion? I can send a car if you're unable to get a ride this late."

Sweat started to trickle down the side of my face at the thought of going back to that place. I remembered it as clear as day, watching it disappear in the rear-view mirror when Wyatt had driven me home. It's an image that'll likely be burned into my brain until the end of time.

"No, it's fine. I can call an Uber and be there later this evening. I'm just leaving work within the next half an hour or so. I do have to pop by my house to make sure the girls are fed, but then I'll make my way down. Is this your personal number, so I can give you a call when I'm on my way?"

"You don't need to call; we'll be waiting for your arrival. I'll have Wyatt keep an eye out for any cars that come through the gate."

"Alright. Thanks so much. Have a wonderful rest of the day."

"You too!"

"Who was that?" Mr. Davis asked, jacket in hand.

"Oh!" I blinked, not realizing he had been standing there. I hoped he had not been there for long. "Just the assistant to my previous employer. Something about some paperwork I forgot to sign when I left."

"I see," he nodded. "Well, I'm off. You have a great weekend. See you bright and early on Monday!"

I fumbled around my desk to grab whatever things I needed as my brain turned to mush. I really hoped that I would not run into Nate while I was there. I had no idea what I would even say to him if we came face to face.

* * *

After returning home and whipping up Nora and Sarah an easy dinner, I bid Nana farewell and gave the twins lots and lots of kisses.

The entire ride there, I did my best to calm my racing heart, but there was no use. I was grateful that the Uber driver did not try to engage in pointless chatter; that would have only made me more nervous. Instead, I just stared out the window and prayed that this night would be over quickly.

"Wow, you used to work here?" the man said as he pulled up to the closed gate.

I did not remember it ever being locked while I was here, but perhaps it was a new security measure. After Alex's meltdown in his father's parking lot, perhaps they were taking precautions for keeping out unwanted visitors. He pressed the silver button, and it beeped a few times before someone answered.

"Hello?" a familiar voice greeted. I recognized it instantly—Wyatt.

"Hi. Yes, I'm here dropping off a Miss Sadie Thatcher," the man explained.

The box beeped two more times and the gate opened. Once he was clear to pass through, he drove the rest of the way until we parked underneath the arch. Wyatt slipped through the front doors dressed in his usual black attire. Seeing him brought a smile to my face. He opened my door and offered a hand, and I happily took it.

"Miss Thatcher." He bowed, making my cheeks hot. "Welcome back to the mansion. Everyone has missed you."

"Aw, that's very sweet of you to say." I'm sure not everyone missed me, but it was still a nice thought. "Am I meeting Jack in his office?"

"Actually, he's a little under the weather at the moment, so you'll be dealing with Nathaniel directly. I hope that's alright."

"Do you want me to wait for you, Miss?" the Uber driver asked through the window.

"It's alright," Wyatt answered. "I'll take her home later. You're free to go."

I watched the car pull away and after a few seconds, Wyatt placed his hand on the small of my back and guided me toward the house. I inhaled through my nose and exhaled through a thin space between my lips, repeating my safe mantra so that I wouldn't pass out.

When he opened the doors, my heart most definitely skipped a beat. The front hall was decorated in pale pink and champagne-colored everything. There were hundreds of bouquets of flowers, balloons wrapped around the banisters of both staircases, and at least an equal number of candles spread out across the floor and on every other available surface. A vintage-style arbor took up the hallway that led to the dining room, and underneath it stood Nate, who wore a black suit.

I turned to ask Wyatt what all of this was about, but he must have slipped back outside, leaving me alone with the man who I once thought was the love of my life. Perhaps he still was.

"I'm sorry for making you come here under false pretenses," he began. "I just wasn't sure if you would come otherwise."

"How sneaky of you," I murmured, taking a step into the foyer. "So, if not for legal purposes, why am I here?"

Nate held out his hand, and with very little hesitation, I walked across rose petals to join him under the arbor.

"I love you, Sadie Thatcher. I'm sure that doesn't come as a surprise to you. I'm sorry that I left that night; I just wasn't sure what else I could do. I knew that I could never be in the same place that you once were, and I did not know if you'd still want to be with me after that. And I'm sorry that I left you to join the army in high school. I wish I could take that back too, but as Jack annoyingly reminded me, we cannot change the past. All we can do is hopefully learn from it, so we don't repeat the same mistakes. And so, Sadie, I have something very important to ask you."

"Wait!" I blurted, and he stopped, his eyes going wide. "Before you do, there's something I have to say, or rather, tell you." I took in a deep breath and mustered up as much courage as I could. "Nora and Sarah are your kids. I found out I was pregnant with them a few weeks after you'd dropped out of high school. I had no idea how to contact you while you were overseas, and so much time had passed since then, I wasn't sure how to tell you once we became reacquainted. I'm sorry. I know I should've told you sooner, but I was just afraid—afraid of getting hurt, and afraid that you'd leave once you found out the truth. But that's not all. I'm pregnant again."

I cupped the tiny little baby bump that was hidden beneath my loose-fitting dress. Nate took a few seconds to absorb this information before picking me up and twirling me around.

"I love you so much, and I love those girls already, and I'm going to love this new baby, too. I know you already know what I'm going to say but, Sadie Thatcher, will you do me the greatest honor by becoming my wife?"

He put me down gently and dropped to his knee before revealing a red velvet box. Inside was a massive diamond ring, the biggest I had ever seen in my entire life.

"Yes!"

Chapter 21:

Nate

It had been a few months since I proposed to the love of my life.

For a second, I had been nervous that she was going to tell me that she did not love me the same way I loved her, but finding out that I was the father of two wonderful children with another on the way? Nothing could ever top the pure and utter euphoria I had felt at that moment. It was as if the stars had aligned just for the two of us, and that fate had brought us together once, and had done it again.

The planning had been nonstop ever since.

Sadie had decided she wanted a spring wedding, and we found the perfect place—our new forever home, just outside of the city in the wide-open countryside. The trees were starting to bloom, and the weather was simply perfect.

A lot else had changed, too. Sadie's boss was gracious enough to allow her to work a couple of nights from home to save her from commuting, and Harvard was more than happy to accommodate when it came to the baby's schedule. It all felt like a dream come true. Nora and Sarah were absolutely in love with the house, and every weekend, we had family game night. Sadie's Nana often joined in, and Jack had come by several times, too. I thanked God above that He had given him more time, so that he could be there to celebrate Sadie's and my special day. Not only that, but I had fulfilled his wish—I had given him great-grandchildren, who adored him.

Neither of us had heard from Alex since the day of my father's arrest. I'm not even sure if he is still in the city or if has moved on somewhere else. All I know is that he does not get a single dime from Jack or the company, and I sleep better knowing that. I don't care if he is my blood—he was no brother of mine.

Nor was he a good friend to Sadie. She told me everything he said that day, from choosing to not give me her contact information, to declaring his love. Both of us agreed we were better off without him.

Although everyone expected us to have a grand wedding, we decided on the complete opposite. An intimate wedding was much more suitable for us, with only our closest friends and family in attendance.

"So, are you nervous?" Benjamin whispered.

He was my best man. We had grown really close over the past few months, and I had kept him on in the company and he was one of our top sales associates.

"Absolutely not. I've been waiting for this day since I was a teenager." I winked.

Lydia stood on the other side of the altar. She and Sadie had become the best of friends in such a short amount of time. Her boyfriend sat with Ben's assistant, Robert. There were also a few family members. Jack and his nurse, sat in the front row, along with Sadie's Nana. Mateo lingered near the back with his wife, and some of Sadie's and my old friends from high school. Nora and Sarah, who had been given the most important job of all as flower girls, decorated the aisle with pink petals and then stood on either side of Lydia.

The music started and everyone turned to watch Sadie come down the aisle. She looked like a goddess, truly—not just because she had that pregnancy glow, but she was the most beautiful woman I had ever known, inside and out. Sometimes I couldn't believe she had agreed to become my wife, for a part of me always felt like I would never be able to measure up to her goodness. Not after all the poor decisions I had made in my life. But I like to think of it as we balance each other out. She's got enough for the both of us.

Gabriel guided her down the aisle, and I could tell he had been crying only moments before, and was barely holding it together now. When she was close enough for me to touch, I held out my hand, and she took it, but not before giving her father a quick kiss on the cheek. "I love you," she said. "I'll always be your little girl."

"And I'll always be with you, right in here," he replied, holding a hand over his heart. He turned to me and proclaimed, "I expect you to take care of her for the rest of your days."

"I will. I promise."

Taking both of her hands in mine, we stood and faced each other, and I lost myself for a few seconds in those enchanting brown eyes.

The music ceased and the minister cleared his throat, preparing to begin the ceremony.

"Dearly beloved, we are gathered here today to celebrate the love of this man, and this woman, in holy matrimony. I would like to begin with the vows, and I'm told you two have prepared your own."

"Yes," I said. "I'll start. Sadie, I never thought this day would come, but here we are, hand in hand, ready to take on this new chapter together, and for the rest of our lives. While I never thought it would come, that doesn't change the fact that I've loved you for over a decade and not once has that flame gone out. It's been you, and it always will be you, for as long as there is air in my lungs and life in my eyes. This I swear."

"Sadie, you may proceed," the minister urged.

"Nate, my whole life, I dreamed of what my wedding day would look like—the flowers, the decorations, the dress, the cake, and everything. For a long time, I was afraid it would never come. My heart has and always will belong to you. During that time while you were away..." she briefly looked at Mateo, who gave a nod of acknowledgment. "I like to think you took a piece of me with you. My heart was never whole until we were reunited, less than a year ago. I promise to love you for all that you are, and that not a day will ever go by where you'll ever question my loyalty to you. We're in this together, as we have always been, until the end of our days, and perhaps even after that."

Lydia sniffled, as did Sadie's Nana and father, but other than that, there was only the silence between us for a few seconds, until the minister continued.

"And now we move onto the declarations of love," he said. "Do you Sadie Thatcher, take Nathaniel Turner to be your husband from now until the end of your days? For better or for worse, in sickness and in health, for as long as you shall live?"

"I do." Sadie smiled.

"And do you, Nathaniel Turner, take Sadie Thatcher to be your wife from now until the end of your days? For better or for worse, in sickness and in health, for as long as you shall live?"

"I do," I said.

"Let us exchange the rings," the minister declared.

I turned to Benjamin, who pulled out the tiny pouch from his breast pocket and handed them over. "That was really beautiful, man," he whispered.

I grinned and gave him a quick pat on the shoulder before facing my soon-to-be wife. I handed her my wedding ring and took hers, waiting for the minister to continue.

"Sadie, we'll start with you. Take his ring and put it just before his finger and repeat after me: With this ring, I thee wed."

She did as instructed, and with a deep breath, said, "With this ring, I thee wed." The gold band slipped onto my left hand with no issue. I hoped that was a good sign that everything was going according to fate's plan.

"Now you, Nate. Repeat after me: With this ring, I thee wed."

"With this ring, I thee wed."

Her wedding band joined her engagement ring, and the two of them sparkled in the sunlight.

I had never smiled for so long in my life, and my cheeks were starting to hurt, but I did not have the power to stop. We grabbed each other's hands and faced the minister for the last part of the ceremony.

"By the power vested in me, I'm pleased to pronounce you husband and wife. Nathaniel, you may now kiss your beautiful bride."

"Happily," I smirked.

Cupping her face with both my hands, I kissed her with my entire soul. Our friends and family clapped and cheered, and I never wanted that moment to end. Breaking apart, we walked together up the aisle, and just like that, Sadie became my wife.

"I love you so much." She beamed.

We slipped into the little chalet behind our estate where the reception was to be held. It was nice that it was just the two of us, even if it was only going to be for a few minutes.

"I love you, too," I said, kissing her on the forehead. "All four of you."

"Have you thought of any names for our little boy?"

She rubbed her belly that had continued to grow with each passing week. Nothing had prepared me for when we found out that we were having a son. It kept me awake most nights, mostly because I was afraid of turning out like my father. Sadie assured me that I would be nothing like him.

"How about Jackson? I thought it might be nice to honor Pops. He is the reason we're all here today, him and his conniving ways."

"I still can't believe he bought my old apartment so that I'd have no choice but to take him up on the job," Sadie laughed.

"Fate works in mysterious ways," I said. "So, what do you think?"

"Jackson is perfect."